TIME HUNTER

KITSUNE

TIME HUNTER

KITSUNE
by JOHN PAUL CATTON

TELOS
.CO.UK

First published in England in 2004 by Telos Publishing Ltd
61 Elgar Avenue, Tolworth, Surrey, KT5 9JP, England • www.telos.co.uk

Telos Publishing Ltd values feedback. Please e-mail us with any comments you
may have about this book to: feedback@telos.co.uk

ISBN: 1-903889-41-3 (paperback)
Kitsune © 2004 John Paul Catton
ISBN: 1-903889-42-1 (deluxe hardback)
Kitsune © 2004 John Paul Catton
Time Hunter format © 2003 Telos Publishing Ltd. Honoré Lechasseur and
Emily Blandish created by Daniel O'Mahony
The moral rights of the author have been asserted.

Typeset by TTA Press
5 Martins Lane, Witcham, Ely, Cambs, CB6 2LB, England • www.ttapress.com

Printed in India

1 2 3 4 5 6 7 8 9 10 11 12 13 14 15

TIME HUNTER

Honoré Lechasseur and Emily Blandish . . . Honoré is a black American ex-GI, now living in London, 1950, working sometimes as a private detective, sometimes as a 'fixer', or spiv. Now life has a new purpose for him as he has discovered that he is a time sensitive. In theory, this attribute, as well as affording him a low-level perception of the fabric of time itself, gives him the ability to sense the whole timeline of any person with whom he comes into contact. He just has to learn how to master it.

Emily is a strange young woman whom Honoré has taken under his wing. She is suffering from amnesia, and so knows little of her own background. She comes from a time in Earth's far future, one of a small minority of people known as time channellers, who have developed the ability to make jumps through time using mental powers so highly evolved that they could almost be mistaken for magic. They cannot do this alone, however. In order to achieve a time-jump, a time channeller must connect with a time sensitive.

When Honoré and Emily connect, the adventures begin.

DEDICATION

For my parents – and their invaluable advice and support.

PROLOGUE 1: THEN

Beneath massive wisteria trees, the three samurai secure their blindfolds, and tilt their heads up to smell the heavy air.

They are dressed in the black garb of stealth, and a tiny crest at their shoulders bears the stylized dragonfly symbol of their Daimyo. Swinging around to face the south, they began their cautious, long-striding run towards their target.

In a clearing, the young maiden awaits her noble lover, the young samurai who is even now slipping away from his wife to honour their clandestine meeting. Her face is coy and modest beneath the fan she holds, her kimono an exquisite pattern of red and white *yagasuri* stripes. She stands upon the narrow wooden bridge, looking over the railing at the irises below. The waters of the pond are dimpled by the first gentle drops of rain.

Two of the warriors burst from the forest, running.

The woman swings her head around to watch them approach. She drops her fan. She hobbles from the bridge, kicking off her wooden sandals as she goes.

Then she drops to all fours, loping away from them at a speed impossibly fast. Faster than the samurai, or anything on two legs, can match. She has almost reached the other side of the clearing when she crawls into the trap sprung by the third samurai. Spiked iron caltrops hidden by the long grass, which snag and rip the flesh of her hands and feet.

The three samurai are on her, pinning her down with staves and halberds. Her human face splits apart, cracking open like ice under pressure, and what is beneath pushes through and howls at the samurai.

PROLOGUE 2: NOW

Before them, the exterior of the Fortuna Love Hotel glowed softly in the smoky Kabuki-cho night. Its over-decorated façade and pastel-coloured neon made it look like the most syrupy, sugary confection Shigeru Yamada had ever seen.

He grinned nervously and took his companion's hand. 'Shall we?'

The Love Hotels were truly marvellous inventions, he thought again. Scattered throughout the metropolis, they were not 'hotels' in the real sense; the guests were all Tokyo residents, and it was not essential to stay the night. They were simply rooms with beds in them. Beds placed conveniently near the bars and the offices, so that the city's harassed workforce had another avenue of stress-relief open to it.

Yamada paid at the discreet hospitality slot. A middle-aged female hand flicked out from the tiny gap at the bottom of the tinted glass window, placing his credit card receipt in the metal tray. There was a whispered 'Thank you' from within.

'It's so hot tonight,' he said, self-consciously, in the elevator. 'So stifling in these clothes, isn't it?'

'A nice ghost story would cool you down,' she said, with a sly smile. 'A true ghost story. Did you know that a couple committed suicide in this hotel? He strangled her and then hanged himself with his own belt. In the very room we're going to.'

His smile ran off his face like melted butter off a knife. 'You're not serious . . . are you?'

She laughed, and reached out to flick his nose playfully. 'It worked, didn't it?'

They had met online.

Yamada had wanted to celebrate his promotion. It was hard to find a girlfriend, these days; organizing the Nagano prefecture dam concession had them all working until nine or ten each night, on what they laughingly called 'voluntary overtime'. The dating websites seemed the perfect answer; post a message, arrange to meet.

She was as attractive as the emailed video-clip of her had shown. Her cosmetics were perfect, her face a cool, untroubled image in porcelain. And her dress; the ragged imitation claw-mark at her shoulder, three slits in the shimmering fabric, tagged it unmistakably as a Hide and Chic original.

A girl of the times.

They slipped off their shoes in the entrance of the refreshingly cool hotel room. A plush maroon bed reclined beneath a huge mirror plating the ceiling. The *karaoke* machine and Game Station glittered in the corner. The bathroom beckoned from the right. He asked the girl to 'make herself comfortable' while he took the shower first. He doused himself with soap, shampoo and conditioner, setting the shower controls from cold to hot and back again, scrubbing away the accumulated smells of the city.

Finally, fresh in his hotel *yukata* robe, Yamada ventured out of the bathroom. 'The shower's great,' he called, softly, 'but perhaps you'd like to join me in trying out the tub?'

There was no reply. The girl was sitting fully dressed on the edge of the bed, her back to him, her head bent over her lap. It looked, for all the world, as if she'd suddenly received some distressing news, and was bowing her head in utter sadness.

'Is everything all right?' The young man sat next to her, reaching out gently to hold her shoulders, turning her around to face him. The girl's head was bowed so low that her long, glossy hair had fallen over her face, completely hiding it.

'What's wrong? You're scaring me.' He reached out to brush the hair away. His fingers parted her fringe – and suddenly recoiled, when they encountered not the soft skin of her face, but more hair, more hair going back as far as – as far as –

Before he could react, she grabbed his head and thrust her face into his, in a rushed, startling mockery of a kiss.

Yamada gasped as his face was shoved into the smothering, shiny curtain of hair. There was no skin he could feel. There was no face. Just more hair, and, as he tried to cry out in panic, a great hank of it was forced down his throat, making him choke. More tresses slid around his neck, like snakes, and started to squeeze.

The young man fell onto the bed and began to flop like a landed fish, the girl holding him down, their kiss unbroken.

PROLOGUE 3: IN-BETWEEN

The Thailand sun was just as hot as Mitsuo Noguchi remembered it. Perhaps hotter.

Noguchi wiped his brow yet again with his handkerchief. His young son Akihira, by contrast, seemed untroubled, his eyes deep and thoughtful as he looked around him, perhaps affected by the sombre atmosphere of the place in which they stood.

The mid-morning sun hung almost directly above the tall marble cross that stood in the middle of the cemetery, giving its white surface an almost blinding sheen. The symbolism was not wasted on Noguchi. As a younger man, he had snapped gold crosses from the chains that hung around sweating necks, he had fired bullets at the plaster saints of the missionary huts. With his comrades, he had laughed at the foreign gods of black-hearted barbarians.

He was not laughing now.

One year, he thought. It had taken the Japanese army one year to build a bridge that connected Thailand and Burma, where engineers had said it couldn't be done in less than five. And they had done it with a workforce of captured soldiers. A workforce that had existed on a daily ration of rice, with a little salt. A workforce that had gradually withered away in the heat, like neglected flowers.

It was said that the number of the dead had been equal to the number of wooden sleepers supporting the railway track.

Many of their cremated remains were buried here; the Kanchanaburi

War Cemetery. Beneath the molten sun, rows upon ordered rows of bronze plaques on low pedestals stretched into the distance. A garden of names engraved on metal, like strange growths pushing themselves out of the soil to reach the light.

A slight movement to his left alerted him to the presence of others. He grinned and bowed formally as he saw who it was. The black *Amerikajin* and his pale lady friend, walking from the direction of the whitewashed stucco of the Memorial Building.

'Lechasseur-san,' said Noguchi, in heavily accented English, after he had bowed to them. 'Do you have the time?'

The black man smiled, and held up his hands. On his left wrist was the heavy, round Elgin military watch. They both laughed politely.

'When I met you in London,' continued Noguchi, 'that was the first time to make a joke in another country's language. You were very kind to laugh at my poor joke.'

It was the previous night that Noguchi had received the message in his hotel. Honoré Lechasseur was in Thailand on business, and was requesting a meeting. Life was indeed strange. Seven years earlier, after the war, it had taken almost a year for Noguchi to track down the mysterious American, then living in London; now it seemed that the favour had been returned, and Lechasseur had gone out of way to seek out Noguchi.

The American hadn't changed at all. Still the same easy smile, his movements and gestures graceful in their economy.

Honoré Lechasseur; the only surviving friend of Don Payton, late of the Texas National Guard's Second Battalion, with no family or relatives that could be traced. Don Payton, whom Noguchi had watched being starved and beaten in the POW camp not so far from where the cemetery now stood.

The Commandant of the camp had ordered that all of the prisoners' watches be brought to him. He had been an avid collector. Swiss, German, American. All of them had been placed on white cloth in the drawers of the dresser in his office. So much time on his hands. Time stolen from the prisoners of war in his charge.

After the war, Noguchi had been spared the misery of prison, and had been returned to a defeated land on an American ship. But it was he who had ended up with the watches in his possession. And his own way of apologising, he had realised in a stroke of inspiration, would be to return them to the families of the men he had helped to kill.

But of Payton's next of kin there had been not a trace.

The watch stolen from Dan Payton had been an Elgin, with a screw-back military case. Like Payton himself, extremely reliable. Payton had taken care of the other prisoners, negotiating with the officers skilfully for more supplies, bribing the Korean guards with what little they had. He had taken the beatings almost calmly, knowing that if he lashed out in anger it would be the end of him.

And the ticking of that watch had outlasted the ticking of his heart.

'It is so good of you to come all this way,' Noguchi said to the new-comers. 'After the years of war, we need decades of kindness to put it right. If men like Payton-san exist, then there is hope. It was . . . a day like this . . . when it happened . . .'

Noguchi looked towards the north, and the river. Noguchi had been on overseer duty when that section of the bridge had collapsed. He could still see it in his mind's eye, he could smell the newly cut wood, he could feel the springy pine as it gave way beneath him.

'I was upside down, with my foot trapped between two wooden struts. I could see the American's face through the water. And I remember his eyes; he was looking at me as if I was some kind of . . . rare insect, and he was putting his hands down to scoop it out of the water.'

Noguchi screwed up his eyes from the sunlight.

'They pulled his body from the river three kilometres downstream, two days afterward.'

'Some things in life will always remain mysteries,' the black man said gravely.

'Indeed. What would the rabbit say?'

'Beg pardon?'

From his jacket breast pocket, Noguchi pulled a slightly discoloured rabbit's foot charm.

'Back in London, you asked me to keep this, Lechasseur-san. You said it brings good luck. And since I have joined the Temple, I have had luck in great quantities. My wife . . . my son. The mercy of Amida Buddha.'

He looked again at his son, and sighed. 'You know, the *Zazen* priests in my country have the tradition of the *koan*. A question with no answer, that serves to guide us towards enlightenment. A question such as – if the rabbit could speak, what would it say?'

'Wouldn't it ask for its foot back?' Lechasseur's companion Emily said, and everyone laughed politely.

With a formal bow, Noguchi held out the rabbit's foot with both hands. 'I give this back now and ask you to remember me, Lechasseur-san. I have had more luck than I deserve in my life.'

Hesitantly, Lechasseur accepted the charm. 'I appreciate it,' he said, returning the bow. 'Luck is maybe something we should spread around.'

When he straightened up, Noguchi became aware of the tension in the attitudes of the two visitors. They were staring in the direction of Akihira, who was standing quietly to one side, trying to read one of the nameplates as if it was the key to a great treasure.

'It's the son,' he heard Emily murmur, and turned his head in time to see Lechasseur nod in reply.

'Noguchi-san', Lechasseur said slowly, 'if you'll forgive me, what are your thoughts on . . . your son's future?'

Noguchi lifted up his handkerchief gently to dab his forehead.

'My son . . . I do not want my family to be part of any more wars. By that I mean land wars, and economic wars.'

By the nearest nameplate, Akihira stared away from them across the cemetery, his little head cocked as if he was listening for something. 'They have re-opened the Yasukuni shrine,' Noguchi said. 'They are holding ceremonies in the place where the spirits of our war dead are enshrined. The ministers are taking their young followers there, and they say they are praying for peace.'

He turned, squinting at the two visitors. 'But we Japanese are very skilful at forgetting what we *choose* to forget. They are redrawing the boundaries, already, and they are rewriting the textbooks. How can they pray for peace, in a shrine dedicated to the spirits of war?'

Noguchi bowed his head. 'I do not want my son to be part of this. I am thinking of enrolling him in the priesthood. I have some friends in Kyoto; they used to be classmates of mine.'

Emily nodded at length, giving Noguchi a smile as radiant as the sunlight that swam around them. 'Noguchi-san, believe me when I say, you've made a very wise choice.'

1: KYOTO

The lightning strikes; a shower of sparks.
In the blink of an eye, you have missed seeing.

Akihira Noguchi, the aged Custodian of Sanjusan Gendo Temple, passed a hand over his face and looked down the corridor once more.

Through the shadows cast by the rows of candles, he could see that the two strangers were still there. Noguchi breathed in deeply, the heady sandalwood of the incense and the deep, throaty tones of the Heart Sutra chanted by the acolytes calming him down. He mentally prepared his speech – his English-language version of the Temple's history – that he had given to countless foreign visitors to Kyoto.

But there was something different about these two. The ghost of a memory. These strangers had aroused something in his heart that he could not explain.

As they walked, they studied with great interest the thousand and one statues of the Goddess Kannon, standing in ordered lines down the length of the long, dark corridor, each one the size of a grown woman. The gold leaf plating their serene faces and armoured bodies cast a golden reflection on every object around them, and transformed the daylight within the temple into a hazy, phosphorescent mist.

Each one had the face of the Goddess; no two faces were alike. Noguchi had often heard visitors remark, as they looked upon the archaic and intoxicating presence, that at least one of the faces resembled a relative who had passed on.

To his surprise, the young lady spoke excellent Japanese. 'Would you be Akihira Noguchi, the Custodian of the Temple?'

'That is so,' he replied. 'Have we met before?'

'We were acquainted with your father.'

'Ah – *naruhodo*. I see. You must forgive me – my father did not speak so much of his trips abroad – it was his modest nature, I'm afraid . . .'

'Modest, yes, you're right. But we did mention that we would call in to see you some day. My name is Emily Blandish, and this is Honoré Lechasseur.'

Noguchi bowed deeply.

'I have a question,' the tall black man asked, his smile broad but betrayed by the intensity in his eyes.

'Please.'

'Why do you have a thousand statues of the same God? I mean, Goddess?'

'Ah.' Noguchi cleared his throat, lifting both his head and his voice as he gestured at the golden images around him. 'They represent the Goddess Kannon, who can manifest herself in an infinite number of forms, and all at the same time. Each head has nine faces upon its brow. Each statue has forty arms, each arm with the duty of saving twenty-five worlds. Each one is the image of Kannon, but no two are exactly alike.'

Noguchi paused. The foreigner's head moved, birdlike, as his gaze flicked from statue to statue. His hand raised itself in an attempt at a gesture, fingers twitching as he became lost in thought.

'It's like . . .' he said eventually, '. . . like looking at the same person, but at different points in time. Each person, manifested a thousand times over, today, tomorrow, before, after, long ago, far ahead. The same person, but never the same. Always slightly different. Changing. Being changed.'

Noguchi smiled in genuine pleasure.

'Lechasseur-san, you show a great understanding of our culture. At all times, in all places, we are ourselves, and we think we cannot be anyone else. But the wonder of it is that we are also the Buddha, and we do not know it.'

Lechasseur opened his mouth, and closed it again, content simply to look around him.

'We would appreciate learning a little more about this place,' Emily said. 'We . . . didn't get much of a chance to study before travelling.'

Noguchi nodded. 'Ah. If that is the case . . . perhaps you would like to see our garden?'

They stepped out of the temple, into the noonday Kyoto heat. The courtyard held only a few visitors, looking around them with polite but distracted interest. The cicadas in the nearby cedar trees chorused in their undulating drone, a sound that the priest had always found aided him in meditation.

Noguchi led them through a miniature gate, into a courtyard shaded by a giant wisteria tree, and waved his hand toward their destination.

The rock garden, constructed and maintained according to the Zen school of Buddhism. The elegantly raked sand glittered in the sunlight. Noonday shadows pooled around the irregular islands of stone.

The black foreigner stared at it with an unreadable face.

'You did say this was a *garden*?'

Chihiro Ishii, also known as Temari, the fourteenth Maiko of the House of Kiyotsugu, composed herself as the silent male assistant began to apply creamy white face-paint to the bridge of her nose.

As was customary, the make-up would be applied to the whole of her face, throat, and back of her neck, and then the assistant would assist her in the nightly task of donning the ceremonial kimono over the thin cotton slip she presently wore.

The Mistress had repeatedly told her that the top bureaucrats from the Ministry of Transport would attend tonight. It was *Yamahoko-Junko*, the height of the Gion Festival, and just about every Government mandarin was in Kyoto to be seen at the Festival.

She sighed as the assistant bent closer, mumbling apologies as he spread the make-up around her face, transforming it into a porcelain, doll-like mask. If someone gets this close to me in the future, she thought again, I don't want it to be a slave of the tea house, or some bigwig salaryman stinking of hair dye and malt whisky. It's going to be a man who's *with it*. One of those surfers she had seen around the city. Or, even wilder, one of those up-and-coming TV talents.

The assistant finished the make-up at last, and then began to assist her with the donning of the kimono. It was an awesome creation. The design of tiny flowers and whirling snowflakes shimmered in the room's soft light, giving the kimono a depth that was difficult to pull one's gaze away from. There at the shoulder was the trademark of the Hide and Chic brand – three tiny claw-marks slashed through the kimono's fabric – exposing her white-painted skin. The spoiler of the kimono's beauty, a reminder of the fragility of worldly life; or so the fashion magazines said. A gift to the house from the Minister of Finance, it had surely cost enough to keep a small business afloat for a year.

The Mistress of the House fluttered her way into the room, her face set in the habitual, hardened expression that she wore out of sight of her clients. 'Aren't you ready yet, Temari? The guests are asking for you.'

'It's my fault,' deferred the assistant, on cue. 'I cannot apologise enough for my clumsiness.'

Temari got to her feet. It was true; the new kimono was lighter than the others. And cooler. In fact, she felt positively refreshed.

Accompanied by the Mistress's background chivvying, Temari shuffled down the corridor, the silver ornaments in her hairpiece jangling like wind-chimes. Accepting the tray of pickled goods from another assistant, she eased open the sliding door and entered the main guest chamber on her knees, holding the tray before her.

The massed applause of the clients and the twanging notes of the *shamisen* awaited her. She set the tray down on a table, bowing deeply. When she raised her head, she saw they were all grinning at her, eyes sly and lascivious; about fifteen men in suits almost identical shades of grey, middle-aged and half-drunk. All of them displayed their customary badges of office; greased-back thinning hair, liver spots staining wrinkled skin the colour of teak, eyes swimming behind thick spectacles, cigarette smoke hissing from between crooked teeth.

The honourable ranks of the Permanent Under-Secretaries to the Minister of Transport.

Cigarette smoke swirled in the room; a room that, through the new kimono, felt surprisingly cold. The air-conditioning's turned up high tonight, Temari thought; one of the clients must have requested it. Or maybe she was catching a fever . . .

Trying to suppress the sudden tremor in her limbs, she shuffled demurely towards her clients, the crystal barrettes in her hair chiming like tiny bells.

In the entrance lobby to the tea house, Hideki Mochizuka breathed deeply, trying to remain calm. His job as a journalist for *Blue Deluxe* magazine had brought him to some exclusive places, but never to a tea-house in the Gion district of Kyoto before. At the humble age of twenty-seven, a son from a corporate white-collar family, and a graduate of a nondescript university, Mochizuka knew how out of his depth he really was. Gion was the preserve of Japan's elite; politicians, company presidents, descendants of illustrious samurai families.

As Mochizuka stood, nervously pretending to admire the artwork of the half-curtain that hung in the open doorway, he heard the shuffle of someone's slippers approaching. He turned, to see the Mistress of the House emerging from the darkened interior; a lady who obviously wasn't pretending to conceal her disgust and irritation at being interrupted.

'If you wish to see Temari, I am afraid that is not possible. Our customers are exclusive, and they do not include magazine reporters. Especially those of the gutter press,' she said, eyeing him up and down.

'With the greatest respect, it's not exactly Temari I've come about. It – it's something concerning her kimono.'

The Mistress arched an eyebrow that looked like it had been carved. 'Usually it's what's under her kimono that clients want to know.'

'The thing is, the kimono may be – ah – defective.'

'Defective? It's a Hide and Chic original! What on earth are you talking about?'

Mochizuka lifted up his head, screwing up his courage, staring the Mistress full in the eyes. 'Whoever wears it may be in *danger*.'

The stunned silence that followed was broken by harsh, discordant sounds from within the house. Furniture being knocked over. A strangled shriek. The Mistress twitched her head around, looking as bewildered as if she had suddenly found her house on fire.

An assistant was in the doorway behind them, his face distraught, flapping his hands at them ineffectually. 'It's the guests – please come, please come quickly – it's the guests – '

Mochizuka shouldered roughly past the Mistress and the assistant, and plunged into the tea house interior. Running past sliding doors and paper walls behind which panicked shadows moved, he nearly slipped several times as his socks fought for traction on the highly-polished wood flooring.

He slid to a halt at a darkened corridor up ahead, where one of the assistants was slumped, looking vacantly downward as if shell-shocked. What looked like steam was pouring out of the open door behind him.

'*Yuki-Onna,*' the assistant was babbling. '*Yuki-Onna,* the *Yuki-Onna* – I saw her – ' The assistant now looked at Mochizuka for the first time, and there were tears in her eyes. 'I saw her, and – and she was *so beautiful.*'

Mochizuka lent into the room, waving aside the mist. It was like stepping into an icebox. His breath instantly condensed, and he shivered at the sudden drop in temperature. As his vision cleared, he stared intently into the room, trying to make sense of what he was looking at.

Before him sat the Permanent Under-Secretaries to the Minister of Transport, their grey suits now an arctic white, their skin frosted over and rimy, their spectacles crusted over with milky layers of ice. Icicles hung from their fingers, their sleeves, the tips of their cigarettes. They were all in the posture of getting to their feet, their faces shocked, mouths open, a silent tableaux of panic.

Frozen solid.

The noise, Lechasseur thought, was even more pervasive than the heat.

It had just turned eight o'clock, and with the early onset of darkness some of the day's heat had lessened. But the *noise*; from loudspeakers strung along the wide Kyoto avenue, there pumped an endless, apparently tuneless barrage of piping flute and drums, its mindless rhythm overlapping everything in the Festival. It underpinned the rumble of the huge floats that moved past, the chanting of the youths who tugged them along, the periodic police announcements that crackled over megaphones, the constant babble of the crowd – everything was loud, but the piped music was louder.

Tonight was 17 July 2020; the night of the *Yamahoko-Junko,* the biggest spectacle in the Gion Festival. The streets were packed with tourists and Kyoto residents out in force, looking on from behind police-manned orange crowd barriers, as the thirty-two *Yama* floats trundled through the streets before them. The floats were huge, boat-like affairs; standing on their spear-lined hulls, towering several metres above the pavement, they were crowded with kimono-wearing dancers and musicians, their hands making archaic gestures at their audience. At the prow of each float, a beefy youth wearing nothing but a loincloth was pounding a complex tattoo on a barrel-sized *taiko* drum.

'A tremendous sight, Honoré. The Gion Festival. Over a thousand years old, you know.' Emily was reading from a guidebook, which she was able to translate effortlessly. 'In the ninth century, there was a plague epidemic sweeping Japan; the first festival was staged as a direct appeal to the Gods for help.'

'If you're right, their help might be needed again.'

They were standing at an intersection of one of the main shopping streets in Kyoto, leading towards the river and the Gion area, which gave the Festival its name. Lechasseur was wearing his usual white shirt, dark trousers and jacket, all covered by a long, black leather trench coat. Emily, ever the one to try to fit in, was wearing a smartly-cut powder blue trouser suit and pale pink blouse.

The whole of Kyoto had impressed Lechasseur: it had been laid out on a grid-like system of streets, reminding him a little of San Francisco, but without the streetcars. Moreover, from anywhere in the city centre, it was possible to look down one of the broad avenues and see the haze-shrouded mountains in the distance; an older and more ethereal presence behind the glass and steel of the city.

It was a city of dreams. Perhaps it was the city of *his* dreams, the dreams that had chased him from New Orleans to London.

Or at least one of his dreams.

Among the floats trundled what were obviously antiquities from Japan's different historical periods; a fire engine, wooden carts, palanquins, others that Honoré could not identify. All of them looked as if they were on loan from museums, pulled by men and women wearing short tunics and bandannas, chanting, '*Yosh -oi! Yosh-oi! Yosh-oi!*' in time with their movements. Police officers on motorcycles trundled in stately fashion beside the procession.

Slurping cold noodles from a plastic bowl, Lechasseur continued to stare at the dancing crowds parading before him, and saw their futures embedded in each and every one of them.

It was his talent. It was his curse.

As a child, Lechasseur had been visited by dreams and visions. After nearly getting killed in wartime Belgium, the visions had increased, both in frequency and in intensity. He now understood that every human being was a nexus point of choices and maybes, a fusion of yesterdays and tomorrows. To him, people were a constantly flickering reel of possibilities, ready to unscroll at any moment like the film in a cine camera.

He could see the future. But only Emily could *get* him there. And she was still a mystery to him.

'I thought most Japanese people were supposed to be short,' he observed. 'Some of those guys over there are taller than me.'

'That's what a protein-enriched diet does for you, Honoré.'

'Last I heard, after they surrendered at the end of the War, they couldn't even get enough rice to eat. Had to mix it up with barley like a kind of gruel. Had no taste and still didn't fill you up.'

'I imagine their fixers must have done rather well in a situation like that.'

'Reckon they did,' Lechasseur said, with a slight grin. 'When they weren't getting shot under the railroad tracks.'

Back in London in 1950 – the place and time that he still insisted on calling home – Lechasseur had leafed through a magazine that featured a series of colour photos taken in Japan. Just like anyone else, he imagined, he had been impressed by their exotic beauty; the women in kimonos, the men in their bizarre Kabuki face-paint. Now, experiencing the abundance of sound, colour and movement around him, Lechasseur felt a distinct uneasiness creep in.

It was as if the images he was seeing were alive, but still exactly that: images. Three-dimensional, moving, speaking, and in colour, but images nonetheless. At any moment, a hand might come and turn the page, just as his own hand had flicked through the pages of that still-remembered magazine; and this pageant that he now faced, this procession of half-drunk humanity, would be peeled anyway, and something else revealed beneath.

But the page remained unturned. The world was still there. Honoré suddenly realised that he'd been holding his breath.

'Everything is happening all at once,' he whispered, hoarsely.

'Anchor yourself,' Emily said, lightly. Lechasseur was almost surprised to hear her reply. He hadn't thought she could hear him. 'Stop squinting at it sideways and just hold on to something. Like these people are doing. They're holding on to the calendar.'

'The calendar?'

'Yes. The festivals, the holidays. The holy days. People are trying to connect with something. I felt it back in England, too.'

Lechasseur sniffed. He closed his eyes, and opened them again. He half expected to see the blank, dingy walls of his room back in London, their familiar emptiness matching the emptiness he sometimes felt inside. But all was still light, colour, movement. Bees dancing before the hive, their complex and ritual gestures telling of tomorrow's pollen.

Emily had just spoken again, but something in the crowd had distracted Lechasseur's attention.

He narrowed his eyes. To his right, behind the next wave of dancers, an odd commotion could be glimpsed. There was a curious glittering in the air, a nimbus of white, a cloudlike aura of crystals blossoming into view.

A rift in the parade opened, as some of the dancers stopped what they were doing and turned round, as if in surprise.

The centre of the cloud of white was a young woman, dressed as an apprentice geisha. Her kimono was the purest white, and, as she spread out her arms to her side, the long sleeves almost brushed the ground. Her face was an inverted white teardrop, eyes and mouth so slight that they were mere flicks of an artist's brush. Around her, an aura of frosty white painted the air, as if she was breathing out a cooling sparkle of tiny white crystals onto the people around her. The crowd cooed in delight.

'It's snowing, Honoré.'

'They do say these Japanese are pretty damn clever.'

A discernable whisper went around the crowd; two words whispered in awe, over and over again: 'Yuki-Onna. Yuki-Onna.'

'What they're saying is Snow Maiden,' stated Emily.

'That figures.'

The *Yuki-Onna* smiled at a nearby child, like a stately Ice-Queen. She approached two policemen, who laughed and smiled back at her, enjoying the show. As she came closer, they actually held out their hands closer to her, like watchmen standing around a brazier that radiated chills instead of heat.

As the *Yuki-Onna* got within touching distance of them, a dishevelled young man suddenly burst from the crowd. '*Abu nai. Abu nai! Mina-san, haiyaku nigero!!*'

The policemen turned toward him, their smiles fading. As they looked away, the *Yuki-Onna* reached out a hand, letting it rest light as a whisper on the arm of the nearest policeman.

The officer screamed and jumped away. There was a clear, white handprint of frost etched onto his arm.

Lechasseur turned to Emily and frowned. 'Would you say that counts as something out of the ordinary?'

'Honoré, we've got to stop her. Whatever she is. If the crowd panics, someone's going to get killed.'

'Easier said than done.' Lechasseur glanced behind him. The attendants of the floats and the Edo-period fire engine had left their posts and were, along with everyone else, hurrying away from the main road, casting worried glances back at the ice-woman. 'Hmmm. I wonder if they'd mind if we borrow that.'

'Excuse me for saying so, Honoré, but I didn't notice anything on fire.'

'Just trust me.' Beckoning her to follow, Lechasseur trotted over to the abandoned fire engine. 'Do you think this thing's got water in it?'

'The guidebook said there's a working demonstration later on.'

'Perfect. I saw enough of these kinds of things in London. Got a chance to help out with one of them once. But I need you to go up there and read those Chinese characters – would you mind?'

Nodding, Emily grasped the ladder and pulled herself up onto the carriage. To the back of the engine was an open panel of levers and colour-coded switches, and she scanned the labels covered with tiny marks and characters..

'How much does this water tank hold?' demanded Lechasseur.

'It says here a thousand gallons.'

'Should be enough. Can you see the pump controls?'

'Something called an impeller water pump?'

'That's it. Start priming it, will you?' Lechasseur tugged a length of hard rubber hose away from its reel on the side of the carriage and coiled it onto the pavement. He peered at the nozzle on the end; about one inch wide. That would have to do.

The Ice Maiden was moving closer, drifting along the pavement like a bad dream, her long, delicate fingers making gestures through the blizzard that surrounded her.

'Okay, Emily, can you tell me what that pump panel's saying?'

'It says you've got a full tank. Do you want full pressure?'

'I'd say that's pretty much what we need. Okay, hit "discharge".'

There was a moment's hissing and gurgling as the hose trembled in his grasp like a living thing. He looked up, and met the gaze of the *Yuki-Onna*, perhaps ten feet away from him. Those exquisite eyes, he noticed, were as white as the girl's kimono. 'Now!'

The water burst from the nozzle as a solid, rock-hard stream, and hit the girl square in the chest. She rocked backwards, and the water was instantly transformed into a fantastically shaped sunburst of ice, glittering rivulets and crowns, a sculpture putting itself together in the chaos of an instant. The ice materialised into a veil over the girl's face and torso, encasing her beauty in a thick, glassy mask.

Lechasseur told Emily to switch off. The water slowed to a trickle, and finally a gentle dripping. In front of the fire engine, there stood a grotesquely-shaped block of ice, about seven feet tall and four feet around. At its heart, the *Yuki-Onna* gazed through the frozen sheets of crystal, a fly stuck in amber.

She was still smiling.

A figure broke away from the crowd of dazed onlookers and ran up to them; Lechasseur recognised the young man who had warned the crowd of the danger. '*Sumimasen*,' the man gasped breathlessly, and then, in English, 'I – have question. I am journalist. Can I talk to you?'

Lechasseur could say nothing.

He had awoken from a frozen nightmare into a sweltering summer dream.

He saw the young Japanese man in front of him ducking down in panic as bloated red paper lanterns exploded above his head. Sheets of flames danced silently in front of Lechasseur's eyes. He saw the same young man on a beach at midnight, sitting with his college friends with their backs to a reeking, abandoned boat, swigging Super-dry beer as they consoled each other over the girlfriends they had lost.

He saw the same man, standing in the middle of an empty city street, looking up in horror at a sky writhing with dark, clotted shadows. *Kannon*, he thought. Kannon. That was the name of the Goddess. A procession of statues stretching backwards and forwards, each one frozen in time. All of them the same. All of them different.

'Hello?' The young man was staring at them, flustered, uneasy, waiting for them to reply. '*Ano* . . . if you have no comment . . . '

'On the contrary,' Lechasseur said, snapping back into the moment. 'You're just the person we'd like to speak to.'

2: TOKYO

They left for Tokyo early on the Friday morning.

Honoré and Emily had tacitly agreed that staying in Kyoto to help the local police with their enquiries would only add to the confusion. It had transpired that some of Japan's finest bureaucrats had been flash-frozen before dinner; but considering that the *Yuki-Onna* had manifested herself in front of multiple witnesses, they assumed that to say the police had their hands full would be an understatement.

Their newly acquired friend, Hideki Mochizuka, had acceded to their wishes. He had invited them back to his hotel, and, after a few phone calls, had informed them that the police had taken the frozen spirit-woman 'into detention' – specifically, placed her in a police garage to thaw – and, although they were searching for the two foreigners who had acted so precipitously, really had no idea where to start.

Mochizuka had respected their wish to remain secret. 'A nod's as good as a wink to a blind horse,' Lechasseur had said, and the young Japanese man had nodded feverishly, as if he had understood.

Their new guardian had turned out to be a twenty-eight-year-old reporter from a weekly magazine called *Blue Deluxe* – 'One of the nation's top five,' he had said proudly, although from his description it seemed that the magazine was one of the less reputable, top-shelf kind. Here we go again, Emily had thought. She still remembered the days when she had first arrived in London, an amnesiac refugee from who knew where, and the more sensational elements of the press had dubbed her 'the girl in pink pyjamas'. She didn't trust reporters. Honoré had explained that not all of them were like the ones she had encountered in London, but she was reserving judgment until she managed to locate a copy of *Blue Deluxe*.

Emily was intrigued by the young man's appearance. He wore a suit made of a smooth, ice-blue material over a silvery shirt and matching tie. His hair looked as if it had been lacquered, teased up into tiny, stiff spikes all over his scalp. Odd, Emily thought; but she had noticed the same hairstyle on plenty of the young men bustling around central Kyoto, and so assumed it must be a current fashion. His features were equally unsettling; his sharp nose, high cheekbones and large eyes looked more Burmese that the Japanese of Emily's imagination.

At Mochizuka's hotel, they had managed to convince the young reporter that they were both working on the same story; that the two of them were private investigators from the UK and USA. That was when he had invited them to Tokyo. Despite their protests, he had insisted that he use his expense account to put them up at another hotel.

'We don't use it up, we get it cut,' he had said. Emily quite fancied the trip, and so hadn't protested too much.

And so Friday morning saw them at the huge, greenhouse-like structure of Kyoto station, boarding the bullet train – a long, slender locomotive with a streamlined head.

Lechasseur looked out of the windows for a while after the train pulled out, but soon the procession of anonymous towns with their uniform, boxlike buildings began to give him nausea. He returned to the matter in hand; the vision that had brought both him and Emily first to Thailand, and now to Japan.

'Summer is usual time for scared stories and hauntings,' Mochizuka was explaining, giving an innovative spin to English grammar. 'This is because of *O-Bon* time. We Japanese have ancestor-spirits come back to hometown in July, August.' He put his hands together in an imitation of prayer, and bowed his head. 'Little bit like your Halloween.'

'So summer's the traditional time for ghost stories in Japan?'

'Yes, yes. Very scared stories make us cold, and give us – *nan, to yuu no* – give us the chicken-skin. But this year most scared ever. This year very scared.'

'How come?'

Mochizuka twisted in his seat, leaning enthusiastically towards his foreign guests.

'*Blue Deluxe* always do good business about ghosts. Strange photographs of *O-Bake* in temples and shrines. But this year, so many. This year, everybody seeing ghosts. Traditional Japanese ghosts, like *Okikusan, Oni-babaa, Nimenonna* . . . they are everywhere. People seeing them in mirrors and the windows of the shops. In the streets and in the big buildings too. See them for a second, and then – they gone.

'And then things began really going to the strange. Murder cases. People have been dead. One guy dead in room of Love Hotel, choked by woman's hair. All hair down his throat and round his neck. Woman asleep in bed, police arrests her, but she don't remember anything. One more, *shacho*-san, president of big construction company, he walks the dog in park when something fall on him. Like big stone smash him into the ground like bug. But police can't find stone.'

Mochizuka stopped, took a deep breath and settled his head back on the white-cushioned headrest. Lechasseur didn't need to be a detective to deduce that the thin sheen of sweat on the reporter's brow was nothing to do with the summer heat.

Upon arrival at Tokyo Station, Mochizuka declared he would take them to an uptown part of the city called Shinjuku, and show them some of Tokyo by car. And so it was that they looked out at the twenty-first century from the interior of an air-conditioned taxi.

Emily noticed that the more they saw, the less Honoré spoke. Which was not a good sign.

At least in Kyoto there had been the comfort of real, natural-looking wood. Now, even that was gone. The city was a labyrinth of steel, glass and plastic, with nothing of any size and shape that could remind Emily of 1950s London. The towers were so tall that she had to tilt her head all the way back to see them properly. Even then, their summits were lost in the sunbursts of an aching sky.

It was important to see this, she told herself. What had been made could never be unmade; this world would be waiting for her, in her own personal future. And yet, in some strange way, she already felt familiar with this type of environment. If only she could remember more of her life before her arrival in London! But, as she stared through the taxi window, all she had was an unsettling feeling of *déjà vu*.

They left the taxi and walked west, to Tokyo City Hall, and the Observation Room that Mochizuka had promised to take them to. It felt, to Emily, like she was an ant crossing a garden patio. The towers around her were doing peculiar things to her sense of scale.

But what made this alien flash and roar even more bizarre was the lack of consistency; every new display of unknown technology had a layer of the archaic just beneath the surface. Police officers, with futuristic weapons and radio receivers clipped to their pale blue uniforms, were patrolling the city on bicycles. Towering three-storey television screens were erected on concrete plazas, across which wafted the stench of raw garbage. Mochizuka had told them that the country had been in an economic depression for almost two decades, but the people looked as well-dressed and well-fed as landed gentry; even the dogs some of them walked wore tiny jackets made of cloth – a pointless extravagance, she thought.

And everywhere, from the cedar trees that lined the avenues, there came the chant of the cicadas. An atavistic hum that underpinned the noise of the traffic and the babble from the massive television screens.

Emily's initial feeling of hostility began to melt in the summer heat. It was replaced by something else – an odd, dreamlike feeling of unreality that she could almost enjoy.

'Honoré, do you see those things they're talking into? They look like what the people in Kyoto had.'

'Those walkie-talkie things? Seems like everyone's got them.'

'Well, I'd hate to be left out, wouldn't you?'

Mochizuka took them to a huge and unbelievably crowded store in the heart of Shinjuku, where young Japanese men in brightly coloured tunics stood outside on the pavement, bellowing the prices of their goods through megaphones. Emily tried not to get too distracted by the shelves of unfamiliar objects around her, concentrating on what had first intrigued her; the devices that Mochizuka referred to as 'mobiles'.

'Look, Honoré, they've even got cameras, games and all manner of other things inside them!'

'Cameras . . . I don't go for that Dick Tracy stuff, myself.'

'Oh do come on. Let's find out how they work.'

Mochizuka, guardian angel that he was turning out to be, put two pre-paid mobile phones on his expense account. Emily stood at the corner of a huge crossroads near Shinjuku train station, holding her phone up and pressing the camera button, turning around in a circle until she got dizzy and had to stop.

She giggled as she played the recorded clip back. A panorama of towering offices and shops, with distracted-looking people doing their best not to look at the camera as they walked around Emily on the street.

'Now we take ride in elevator,' Mochizuka invited, 'and look down on city from Heaven.'

The elevator ride up was swift, smooth and silent, but Lechasseur was disturbed by the sensation of his ears popping with the change in pressure as they neared the forty-fifth floor.

The doors opened, and along with dozens of quietly chattering visitors, Lechasseur and Emily found the metropolis of Tokyo spread out before them, beyond the huge windows that lined the room.

On the bullet train and in Kyoto, Lechasseur had talked with Emily of a film he'd seen before the War, before he'd been sent to England with the US Army. *Things to Come*, an adaptation of the book by Wells that he had later avidly read, along with many others. Venerable British actors in odd monochrome robes, regaling the audience with their awkward, mock-Shakespearean speeches about progress. That was how he had thought about the future; flying cars, rocket-packs, trips to the moon and back.

He had seen none of these things. And now this . . .

What had they done? What had happened to this city? Where he'd come from, the British had been talking about 'planning'; it was the great panacea, it was the answer to everyone's problems.

But he'd seen the craze extending to the homes of his Cockney contacts, the areas left untouched by the War, as if the planners had been finishing the job that Goering and his fly-boys had left half done. LONDON CAN TAKE IT, the posters had said; but maybe there was something that it couldn't take.

From what Mochizuka was saying, the people of Tokyo had done this to themselves. They had torn down almost everything after a few years and replaced it with something new – just because it was new.

Lechasseur saw again, in his mind's eye, the garden that the old priest Noguchi had shown him in Kyoto. A garden of stone and gravel.

'But what is it?' he had asked.

'It is a *zen* garden. It is the world around us. Within a box.'

'But there's nothing growing. Nothing alive.'

Again, Lechasseur looked out upon a garden in a box; a dry garden of stone and shadow.

He turned to Mochizuka, trying to break his apprehensive mood. 'Look, apart from waiting for that girl in Kyoto to thaw out, haven't we got any other goods? Anything else to go on?'

'Ah . . . yes. The Kyoto geisha, she had received a very special kimono. A Hide and Chic kimono.'

Lechasseur cut himself off before he could ask the obvious question, one that would possibly blow his and Emily's cover story. Instead, he simply nodded, letting Mochizuka continue.

'And other peoples have been going to the strange recently. *Okashiku nachatta.* Not sleeping, not eating, fighting with their families members. To my interest, everyone had recently made a purchase from Hide and Chic. A dress, a jacket, or perhaps an accessory. Their family and relatives all mention this.'

'They thought it particularly . . . worthy of mention?'

'To buy one of the most exclusive brands in the whole of country? Wouldn't you remember it?'

'How long has this . . . Hide and Chic been operating?'

'Just under a year. They are an incredible success story. Nobody in the fashion world had heard of them, or their president, a woman named Ikari. But they set up their store with a huge loan from several Japanese banks, and when they brought out their first range of goods, they got extraordinary reaction.'

'Extraordinary?'

'*Sugoi, yo.*'

Lechasseur puffed out his cheeks, blowing out air into the Observation Room's dry atmosphere. 'So, in your professional opinion, Mochizuka-san, what would you say was the next step?'

Mochizuka grinned. 'Their winter fashion show is going on for the whole summer. Every Friday and Saturday. Tomorrow is Saturday . . . and *Blue Deluxe* has been sent tickets for the show.'

In the hotel room next to his, Emily, he knew, lay sleeping.

Lechasseur took a bottle of mineral water from the mini-bar, pulled a chair up next to the window, and waited for the morning to come.

Outside, Chinese characters in all colours of neon were crawling up the faces of the dark slabs of the buildings outside, winking in and out of the night, on and off, on and off. They never stopped. The city showed no sign of giving its inhabitants any peace.

They had taken dinner with Mochizuka and been introduced to his boss and his colleagues. They had eaten *sushi*. Lechasseur wasn't averse to the taste – he'd had enough whelks and cockles fresh from Billingsgate to acquire an adventurous spirit when it came to seafood. The only thing missing were the Cockney stevedores spitting out eel bones onto the floor.

But it was the colours that he found less appealing. They were too rich, too vibrant, as if the little parcels of seaweed, rice and fish were considered more to be artform than to be food.

Sighing, he pulled a packet of tissues from his pocket, tissues that someone on the street had been handing out. Among the Chinese characters scrawled over everything, there was a photograph of a perky young businessman with hair like Mochizuka's, and next to it the slogan, in English: *Let's Skills Up!*

He took another sip of water. What he'd seen of the country so far led him to consider that he was in a place where people's bizarre behaviour was regulated by meaningless signs. It was like falling into one of Kafka's bad dreams.

Back in Kyoto, as Lechasseur had stood there goggling at the garden, Noguchi had handed him a rake. 'Here. Tend the garden with this.'

'What for?'

'I always find it good meditation.'

Lechasseur had gingerly traced a wave-like pattern in the gravel. If the sound of the rake, and the pattern it made, was supposed to be relaxing, it hadn't worked.

He had raked over the gravel several times more, until the pattern pleased him better. Then, noticing Noguchi watching him intently, he had passed the rake back with an embarrassed shrug.

'So patterns we make can be remade,' the priest had commented.

'The first one was . . . ugly.'

'So, you begin to understand . . .'

Lechasseur had suddenly remembered something. 'If the rabbit could speak, what would it say?'

'I'm sorry?'

'Your father asked me that, Noguchi-san. Said it was something called a *koan*.'

'Ah. Ah. I see.'

'Do you?' Lechasseur had swept another line into the gravel. 'I wish I did.'

In the hotel room, he now snapped to attention.

For a second, the city beyond the window ceased to exist. In its place was something else. The skyscrapers were melted into stubby, shattered blocks of concrete, their walls mutilated by twisted girders sticking out of them like broken bones piercing flesh. Shadows rippled across a sunless sky. Somewhere in his head, a door slammed. Then there came the howling of a thousand animals, and the floor beneath him shook with the stamping of massive feet. He shivered.

This was the vision that had brought him and Emily over seventy years into the future; the vision that he'd first had in London, when Noguchi the elder had handed him Payton's watch. Payton. Noguchi. Noguchi's son the priest. Everything is connected. If the rabbit could speak, what would it say? What could it tell you?

The vision was gone; the neon was back, and what passed for consensus reality in this city was back in force. But Lechasseur knew that possibilities were circling around them, getting a little closer all the time, like vultures. Continuums were being chosen. The reel of the city's life was ready to unspool.

Lost in thought, he hadn't realised that the sun was coming up. One by one, outside, the neon symbols were flickering out; and a new day was being forced out between the skyscrapers.

3: AOYAMA

Mochizuka, as good as his word, turned up at the hotel on Saturday morning – this time, in his own car – to ferry them to their appointment.

The fashion show was held in an area called Aoyama, and, as they turned off the main freeway onto a long, tree-lined avenue, the travellers looked out at the stores that glided past, merging into one long, unbroken ribbon of glass and metal, names painted in minimalist streaks of black and white.

They turned again, into one of the side-streets, and parked. Here, the streets were smaller and less crowded, possibly because the stores were more of the high-hat, expensive kind, Lechasseur noted. The reporter began to lead them around the corner from the parking lot, but before they got very far, Emily suddenly stopped in her tracks.

Lechasseur turned. Emily was now striding back, towards the end of the narrow street. 'Honoré,' she called, 'come and look at this.'

He shot Mochizuka an apologetic look, and followed Emily. She was approaching a building behind antique zelkova trees in full leaf, a building that looked considerably older than its surroundings.

Following Emily, he found himself passing through a tall, strangely-shaped gate painted bright red, and beyond that, coming to an ancient-looking shrine. At the front of the shrine building, above the offering-box, hung one of the Shinto amulets of which he'd seen so many in Kyoto, made of twisted paper and covered with arcane Chinese characters.

What struck him most were the statues on either side of the offering-box. Large, predatory beasts, carved out of heavy, grey stone, crouched as if to protect the shrine from intruders. The stone looked extremely old, but the shocking white paint daubed on the eyes and snarling teeth of the statues was fresh, and gave them a look of barely controlled ferocity. There were patches of bright red cloth tied around their necks, that looked for all the world like bizarre children's bibs.

'What is it?' Lechasseur breathed. He noticed that his voice sounded strangely muted in the atmosphere of the shrine. The sound of traffic from the avenue close by seemed impossibly distant. In reply, Emily advanced and stretched out a hand, and then stepped back.

'There's something here.'

Honoré tried it for himself. It felt, as he walked toward the statues, like he was walking through cobwebs. Frail, invisible tendrils crackled across his skin momentarily and were gone.

'Something has opened and closed,' Emily mused. 'What is this place?'

'It is *Inari-jinja* – the shrine to the Fox Goddess.' Mochizuka had appeared at the gate. 'It is not so unusual. There are shrines like this all over Tokyo.' He coughed discreetly. 'We can look at more like this one later.'

Their destination was part of what the reporter called a 'mini-mall'. Set back from the road, it consisted of cubes of metal and smoked glass, their interiors little more than murky shadows. A pathway of wooden boards guided them to a set of sliding doors, with a tiny monochrome sign announcing that they had arrived at the main offices of Hide and Chic.

Just like at the Gion Festival, the noise inside hit Lechasseur first. Strident, and as all-encompassing as the stark white walls that surrounded them. He struggled to make sense of it. It resembled jazz, but a jazz based totally on percussion, all other instruments stripped away. It was the bare bones of jazz, chattering snares and pounding bass. It sounded like metal objects being hurled about in a wind tunnel.

An assistant with glowing, over-moisturised skin and wearing a tight and revealing cocktail dress took their passes, and showed them downstairs to their seats. On a long, straight catwalk, models were strutting to and fro with deliberate, exaggerated strides, their elaborately made-up faces haughty and intimidating. The audience regarded them passively from their seats pulled up close to the catwalk, fanning themselves with Hide and Chic brochures, their faces as sullen as poker-players.

The assistant seated the three newcomers next to another foreigner; a youngish black man in a military-style jacket dotted with sequins, a pair of black drawstring pants, and a black pillbox hat the colours of the Ethiopian flag. He nodded a greeting, and regarded Lechasseur hawkishly as the older man sat down.

'Hello, brother,' he said, with a barely discernable American accent. 'Virgil Tutwiler, from *The Time is Now* magazine.'

'Honoré Lechasseur, from, erm . . . *Blue Deluxe*. Care to tell us a little about the show?'

The fashion critic smacked his lips like Lechasseur had just handed him caviar. 'Ikari,' he began, 'is one of the bravest designers in Japan today, perhaps the world. You see how she works with the traditional elements of a culture – in this case, kimonos, belts, tunics and skirts – and takes them into the new millennium?'

Lechasseur looked.

He saw kimonos ripped down the front to expose the model's breasts. Padded shoulders with lumps taken out of them with teeth and claws. Unfinished frocks with sleeves ripped off and then sewn back on in the wrong places.

Just to accentuate the effect, each of the models had red slashes painted diagonally across her face, as if something had marked her with its claws.

'So, what are they going to look like when they're finished?'

Tutwiler snorted in reply. 'These clothes are just *flying* out of the stores. It's all about lifestyle choice, Mr Lechasseur. It's about making an individual statement, one that says I can choose my exploitation, one that says I'm a victim and I don't have to be ashamed of that. My choice of clothes reflects the chaos and asymmetry of my own life. It deconstructs the traditional fashions we have been handed down, and says we can be proud of being the frail flesh and blood that we all are, beneath the clothes.'

Lechasseur exchanged looks with Emily. Me neither, she seemed to be saying.

Abruptly, the house lights came on, announcing the end of the show, and a strikingly attractive woman walked onto the stage to receive a huge bouquet of flowers. 'Ikari,' Mochizuka muttered. The audience rose as one to give her a standing ovation.

'I must fly,' Tutwiler fussed. 'I must squeeze backstage and see what I can pick up. It's been a pleasure, Mr Lechasseur. I'll look out for your work. Tell me, are you specializing in asymmetry, or in distressed fabrics?'

Lechasseur blinked. 'I do a nice line in nylons, when I can get my hands on them.'

Tutwiler looked like he was going to say something, but thought better of it and just reached over and squeezed Lechasseur on the arm.

'Tell me,' Emily said gravely to Lechasseur, as they moved away, 'are you specializing in deconstruction, or in asymmetrical fabrics?'

'If I knocked that joker's hat off, that'd look pretty asymmetrical.'

Mochizuka was beckoning them over to him, with a curious flapping gesture of his hand. '*Hora* – we have talk with Ikari. Come on, please! She have many appointment, crazy busy. Yes, yes.'

Ikari was working the crowd effortlessly and patiently, exchanging a few words with each sycophant before sliding gently into the embrace of the next, until her path through the starry firmament of the fashion world drew her into the orbit of the perspiring Mochizuka and his guests. She approached, wearing one of her own creations, Lechasseur guessed – a kimono with a polyester *obi* and rainbow-coloured pouch, tattered ribbons of fabric hanging down from her back as if she'd been flayed.

He had hoped that her life would unreel before him when they met, that he would be granted some insight into the heart of Hide and Chic. To his disappointment, he had no visions – but still, there was something immensely disquieting about the designer. Her face, classically Japanese in proportion, was attractive without being exactly beautiful, and her cosmetics gave her skin the fairy-like sheen of a new moon.

But deep in her eyes, eyes that were so brown as to be almost black, there was something submerged. Something that glittered darkly beneath the surface. She smiled at her visitors. Her perfume made Lechasseur think of wood and freshly cut hay.

'I'm always delighted to meet guests from overseas,' she gushed, in flawless English. 'And always glad to get attention from *Blue Deluxe*, of course.'

'*Yorishuku onegai shaimasu*,' Mochizuka replied with a bow. '*Go-shokai o-shimasu* . . . Honoré Lechasseur and Emily Blandish.'

'Charmed. What do you think of today's show?'

'Most interesting,' Emily stated. 'But, in all honesty, I can't see the reason for your success, in aesthetic terms.'

'No.' Ikari accepted a cigarette from a flunky and took her time in lighting it. 'In fact, Miss Blandish is quite right. That is the whole point of Hide and Chic. The reason for the brand's success is that it is successful. Once beyond a certain point, the brand spreads like a virus. We know, and so do our rivals, that public image is more important than self-respect. The difference is that we are not ashamed to admit it.'

'That seems a rather cynical view of your customers,' noted Emily.

'Not necessarily. The need to conform is something that cannot be easily denied. Whatever you wear, whatever you look like, people are going to judge you.'

'Reckon that's true,' Lechasseur contributed. 'But whether or not I care about their judgment is a different matter.'

'But still, judgment is a force that should not be underestimated,' she said, sweetly. 'So what do your clothes say about you, Mr Lechasseur?'

'What would they say?' He shrugged. 'Something like . . . he buys his annual suit at Burton's, who are, as people say, the "Tailors of Taste". If the cash is coming in, then maybe Cecil Gee, for something a bit sharper. I'd probably look good in a zoot suit, if there wasn't a law against it.'

'He means a law against the zoot suit,' put in Emily. 'Not against him looking good.'

Ikari narrowed her eyes. 'How totally charming. And you?'

'Oh, I'm afraid I can't stand here in your offices and claim to be stylish myself,' sighed Emily. 'After all, style works on a number of different layers, doesn't it? Some people would want to express their personalities through what they wear. Others just take it as another trend to be followed. But others would turn that right around, into something else entirely.'

'Meaning what?'

'Meaning that some people become very skilful at disguising who they really are.'

Lechasseur watched Ikari's eyes widen suddenly, and the smoke from her menthol cigarette leak out slowly from between her teeth. 'Yes,' she said, eventually. 'Perhaps none of us is what we seem. Well, if you will excuse me, a hundred people are waiting to undress me. Technically speaking.'

And with that, she was gone, drifting away through a crowd of admirers and press.

At the door, as they were about to leave, someone stopped them. One of the models, with a formal Japanese bow, handed each of them a silky garment wrapped in clear plastic. 'Ikari asked that you be given these.'

'You serious? What are they?'

'Souvenirs of your visit. Jackets for the men, a dress for the lady. She said you must have travelled *very* far to be here.' The model hesitated, and then pushed her face close to Lechasseur, almost as if she were *sniffing* him. 'You must be very tired.'

And then the girl strutted away on ludicrously high heels, giving Lechasseur no time to hand back the gift. The big man turned slightly; Mochizuka's mouth was open so wide that it was as if his jaw had forgotten that it had a hinge.

'You see this? She give us Ikari original! *Shinjirare nai!*'

Emily was already out of the mini-mall. Lechasseur was behind her, the wrapped jacket flapping as he carried it over his arm. 'What the heck was all that talk about back there?'

'There's something wrong about her,' Emily snapped. 'Mochizuka was right. She knows what's going on, that's for certain. Didn't you feel something?'

'Yes. Sure did. But I can't explain it. What did you sense? Is she like Mestizer; another traveller?'

'No. They're both creepy, but Ikari's creepy in a different way. She . . . I don't know how to put this. She . . . smells funny.'

'Hey, now, I know she criticised your dress sense, but . . .'

'No, really, it's like a . . . scent. Like something she's done to herself. And did you notice her breathing? Something peculiar about it. Very peculiar.'

Mochizuka caught up with them just as they reached his car. He deactivated the car alarm, inadvertently startling them with its musical chiming sound, and opened the doors for them. Lechasseur tossed his gift jacket in casually and got in the back seat after it.

'Aren't you going to put on?' Mochizuka spluttered.

Lechasseur frowned, peering at the jacket's fur-trimmed lapels and shimmering fabric, scowling at it as though it was going to jump up and bite him.

'No, maybe not. Reckon it's not my size. Now, then . . . let's take another look at that shrine to the Fox Goddess, if you don't mind.'

4: ASAKUSA

As the day grew older, Tokyo stewed in the heatwave. Overworked air-conditioners fouled the streets outside with their metallic, pumping breath. Salarymen trotted from office to office, jackets over their arms and handkerchiefs pressed to their brows. Office ladies smoked menthol under their parasols, faces glowing beneath layers of UVR-proof cosmetics.

The back of Lechasseur's shirt was already drenched, and Emily was fanning herself with a map of the area she had picked up from an information point. Above their heads, a giant paper lantern hung, dominating the weathered wooden gate through which an endless stream of limp, harassed-looking onlookers was passing. Must be ten foot tall, Lechasseur thought, and six foot around. Carved on either side, fearsome Buddhist demons scowled at him, their stone jaws and wild, staring eyes blackened and pitted with age. *Kaminarimon*; the Thunder Gate. Mochizuka had brought them to Asakusa, the oldest part of the city.

The reporter bowed, indicating the gate with a stiff-armed gesture. 'Please.' Lechasseur leading, they entered the grounds of Sensoji Temple.

They found themselves in a long, narrow avenue that stretched on into the gathering dusk. On either side were stalls jammed together, above each one, flowery starbursts of Chinese characters declaring its name. The surfaces of the stalls were filled to overflowing with things that Lechasseur struggled to identify. Dolls with blank, staring faces. Masks of *kabuki* actors, laughing demons, cartoon animals. Thin cotton robes. Miniature notebooks of rice-paper. Kites the size of Lechasseur's hand, with dragons painted upon them. Brush paintings of misty mountain landscapes. The air was full of the chiming of the wind-bells hanging from the canopies of a dozen stalls, and the aromas of grilling meat mingled with the ever-pervasive incense. Elderly men and women, creases in elaborate webs around their eyes and mouths, clapped their hands together and bellowed '*Irrash-ai! Irrash-ai!*' at the passers-by.

Lechasseur was beginning to like it.

'I thought that was a smile on your face I saw,' commented Emily.

'You know what? This place kind of reminds me of home. Got that same kind of downtown mercantile feel to it. I don't think this place has changed much over the years, because it feels like the people here don't give a damn.'

'There might even be some fixers still here for you to hang around with, Honoré.'

'Yes, well, don't get me wrong.' He frowned. 'Most fixers are bad people sometimes doing good things.'

'We have special thing here,' Mochizuka explained to them. 'In pagoda up ahead, there is holy image of Buddha. Very special, very secret. Nobody can be allowed to see that.'

'Well, if nobody's allowed to see it, how do you know it's still there?'

Mochizuka's smile slipped for a second, then returned full force to beam at the American. 'Oh, you joking. We *know* it is there.'

They walked slowly down the long avenue, easing their way through the crowds, their senses almost overwhelmed by the relentless assault of the arcane rubbing shoulders with the trivial. Before them, the dark mass of Sensoji Temple itself grew against the twilight sky, its burnished wooden mass seeming to gather what little light remained and absorb it into its hidden, inner sanctums.

That would be the high tide mark, Lechasseur thought to himself. That would be the rock on which the wave of modernity finally broke and washed back into the uptown city. Leaving these people here, in their own little rock pool, busy fighting to live their own lives and make up their own minds.

Lechasseur took a deep breath of the incense-laden air, turned around slowly to appreciate the bustling scene around him. He stopped, stared hard at one of the stalls behind him.

Three figures were standing motionless by this particular stall, ignoring the crowds around them, just staring back at Lechasseur. In their cotton *yukata* robes and wooden sandals, they were unmistakably female. Their faces were covered with cheap plastic masks from the stalls around them, flashing white teeth and grotesque, bulging eyes, like cartoon faces of dogs.

Or foxes.

'*Do shita no?*' Mochizuka's voice, beside him. 'Are you all right?'

Lechasseur glanced at the reporter. 'Yes, but there's – '

The women had gone. Disappeared.

The day seemed to have suddenly grown colder, and the air thicker. 'Emily, did you see something out of place just then?'

'No. Should I have done?'

'I'm not sure.' He sniffed, rubbed his chin. 'But I've got a feeling that coming here maybe wasn't a waste of time.'

At the entrance to the main Temple was a huge incense-burner, where a line of visitors waited to lean forward into the smoke, believing it would bring them good health. Mochizuka led them up to the wooden gate, tossed a few coins into the collection box, and asked them to bow their heads in prayer.

'We say prayer,' he explained. 'Spirits watch over.'

At the rear of the Temple compounds, down a short driveway and through an archway covered in garish lettering, lay their destination. Hanayashiki Amusement Park. The oldest funfair in the city, and also the smallest. Above the archway hung a familiar red, horned, demon-head, but this one grinned inanely at the people entering below.

'Shall we go in?' asked Mochizuka.

Lechasseur walked into the most cluttered space he had ever seen. It looked as if someone had taken the basic idea of a fairground, with merry-go-round, painted rockets and sea-animals, futuristic towers of shining metal, and wound it around itself so that it could squeeze into the smallest space possible.

There was an explosive sound of screaming overhead, and Lechasseur looked up sharply. Metal carriages, carrying people waving their arms and shrieking with laughter, were shooting along a rickety-looking elevated railroad. From the opposite direction, what looked like a pirate ship carrying more children flew into view, suspended by a thin monorail above the gondola.

'You were wondering where the flying cars were, Honoré,' commented Emily, wryly.

'I wish I hadn't asked. I feel like I've just drunk a whole jug of moonshine. Where do they keep the pink elephants?'

'I've no idea. But we could ask Red Riding Hood and Mr Wolf; they're over there on that cakewalk thing.'

They walked further into the park, Lechasseur's eyes trying to keep track of all the things that swung, flew, rocked, and bobbed around him. It was enough to make him remember the days when he had continual headaches.

A little further on, past tiny wooden kiosks selling steaming food in improbable shapes and colours, a massive white concrete building stood. People were waiting there in queues that wound around the first and second levels, eager to board what was obviously the rollercoaster. Eager, thought Lechasseur, to get catapulted around a space not much bigger than my London bed-sit.

The connection was foxes. When they had been working at the offices of *Blue Deluxe* that afternoon, looking up information on the Inari shrines around Tokyo on one of their astoundingly compact 'computers', Emily had found a story filed two weeks earlier. It had concerned a nest of urban foxes in downtown Tokyo. Food going missing, animals glimpsed from windows at night, strange noises coming from the park after it had closed at the end of the day.

'There are foxes making a lair in this place called Asakusa,' Emily had said.

'And there's a nightingale singing in Berkeley Square?'

It was always good to see Emily smile. Her face, framed with long dark hair, would light up in a way that was guaranteed to lift his spirits. But his experiences as a fixer in post-war London told him that no detail could be overlooked. Because it was precisely that small detail that could come back and find you, usually with a gun or a knife.

Mochizuka stretched out an arm and pointed, and Lechasseur turned to look. The reporter was indicating a building to their right: a fake promontory of rock three stories high, overgrown with plastic-looking vines and creepers. A wooden, Japanese-style bridge led up to a doorway above their heads. The sliding door had holes ripped in its paper screens, gaping like dark mouths.

'The manager says that they've heard things around that building. Seen things moving.'

'And that building is . . . ?'

'It is the *obakeyashiki*. The haunted house.'

'Why is it that nothing surprises me anymore?' Lechasseur studied the building, wiping the sweat from his brow. 'So what we're looking for is in the scariest place in the park?'

Mochizuka shrugged. 'Rumour is good for the business, seems like.'

'You go and have a closer look,' Emily told Lechasseur. 'I'll walk around and see if there's anything else. See you by that big plaster gorilla in, say, thirty minutes?'

Stepping warily onto the rickety wooden bridge, Lechasseur and the reporter eased past the dozen or so people waiting to enter, and stood beneath another leering demon-face staring down at the park's customers.

'You want to go in?' Lechasseur asked.

'But it is very scared. You know . . . ah . . . anyway, how about you?'

Lechasseur shrugged. Judging by the general expressions of the people leaving by the exit a few yards away, there didn't seem to be anything untoward in there to see. 'Maybe some time when it's not so crowded.' He pointed at something painted in white on the dark, age-stained wood below the grinning demon-head. 'What's that supposed to be?'

The smudged, ghostly-white figure resembled a horned, shaggy dragon, its forelimbs rearing up menacingly. On its flanks were rows upon rows of what seemed to be wide, staring eyes, gazing blindly down at the heads of those waiting to enter.

'It is . . . ' Mochizuka paused, searching for words. 'It is *Hakutaku. Setsumei ga dekinai. Gomen nasai*, Lechasseur-san, I cannot explain.'

From beyond the door came muffled shrieks of delighted fright.

The park was too much, Emily thought. It was too bright, too small, there were too many things going on.

If there really were urban foxes here, she thought, everybody seemed interested in them. There were references to them in the scattered threads of conversation she heard around her. It was a bedtime story. Like children scaring themselves by holding up spiders that they'd found in the garden.

Something came into her peripheral sight and made her look up; a gondola cruised overhead, carrying three or more children, their narrow Asian faces grimacing as they looked down on her.

Is this how Honoré sees things?, she wondered. Is this how he sees the world when he has his visions? An endless flow of images, all of them fighting for his attention? A barrage of things so fleeting that all meaning gets washed away in the current?

Time seemed little more to her, at the moment, than a process of endless flow and spillage. If there was a meaning to things, if there was a reason for all this, if there was a God, surely it must appear and disappear before it could ever be grasped. And her existence was perhaps the most meaningless of all. Someone who could walk through the cracks in the world and be everywhere. Be part of everything. But no memory. No history, no progressive, organizing force that had brought her to this moment. She was just . . . here. But then there were the tormenting flashes of her past life, of a man she had travelled with, who had rescued her . . . and of demons, horned beasts and monsters beyond imagining. No wonder she liked to stay over at Lechasseur's flat, to know that when she woke in the night, sweating from another forgotten dream, there was someone there who cared and could comfort her. Something was coming, and she hoped it would take its time about it.

Beyond a shooting gallery, with a row of paper lanterns and plastic flowers hanging over its canopy, was a tiny window marked Fortune-Telling.

And why not?, she thought. Why am I here? Why not ask.

The woman beyond the window was not extravagantly dressed, like the seaside gypsies of England. She was wearing a modest, long-sleeved kimono, her hair up and held with rainbow-coloured hair pins. Her face, meticulously made-up behind old-fashioned reading glasses, was beginning to look buttery with age.

'What can you tell me about myself?' Emily asked. It came out a little more boldly that she'd intended.

'How would you like me to tell you? The lines of your palm? The shape of your face? The characters of your name, in *katakana*? The yarrow sticks?'

'What are the sticks?'

'See for yourself, young lady. If you want rice cakes, it's best to go to the rice cake maker.' The woman held up an old rectangular tin, and rattled it under Emily's nose. It made a noise like dice inside a cup. 'Choose.'

Emily put her hand in the tin, feeling long, slightly sharp objects poke her fingers. She pulled out two long wooden sticks, each with a tiny number painted on it.

'Four and nine,' she read.

'Ah. Now, let me see . . .' From a within a velvet bag, the old lady produced two scraps of stiff Japanese paper. Unfolding them, she began to read.

'The number four. Something buried, but partially alive. Strong hearts, and old fears. Moons falling out of the sky.' She sucked in air through her teeth, and delivered her final judgment. 'Beware of men wearing red.'

Emily frowned.

'And number nine?'

Another tiny rustle as wrinkled fingers daintily peeled open the augur. 'Everything is fractured. A messenger will come from your past, riding a bird of prey.' She peered at Emily through her reading glasses. 'The hunting mouths are hungry.'

'Yes. Quite. But what does it mean?'

'What does it mean? What does it mean?' said the woman, in mock outrage. 'What is the face of the Buddha, when asked three times?' She screwed up the augur in her fist, and then opened her palm, holding it out towards Emily. 'Look for yourself.'

Emily looked. The paper, screwed up into a ball by the old woman's hand, was slowly and silently unfolding itself.

'Oh,' she said.

It was vast. There was so much that had been folded up inside the paper, endless corridors, time and space redrawn in endless patterns. She felt the first wave of vertigo, as she began to fall into the patterns, but it was too delicious and frightening to stop.

'Oh,' the fortune-teller repeated, in a flawless copy of Emily's own voice.

It was time for the park to close. Lechasseur and Mochizuka watched families and couples walk past them as the day ended and night began to wrap itself around the park. They waited beneath the giant plaster gorilla, trying to make small talk last as long as it could.

Emily didn't show up.

Eventually the staff stood in front of them, making their formal bows.

'*Moshiwake gozaimasen, okyaku-sama* . . .'

Finally the manager returned, and had a short conversation with Mochizuka. 'Seems like everyone has go out from park now. Are you sure Emily said to meet here?'

'Yes. By King Kong here, I'm absolutely sure.'

'*Sore ja* . . . maybe she already go out?'

Lechasseur took a few steps forward into the park. The only people to be seen were the uniformed staff, moving from attraction to attraction, with the distracted expressions of mothers putting away toys.

'Emily,' he said, in a voice only loud enough for himself to hear.

'Emily . . .'

5: THE OBAKEYASHIKI

Emily eased herself out of the strangest dream. It was a confused, chaotic dream, full of running and screaming, figures glimpsed through driving rain and mists. No change there then.

She stretched a hand up to rub her eyes. She was lying on her back, the smell of incense and mildewed straw matting all around her. She sat up; she was in a large, unfamiliar room, Japanese style, bathed in the half-light glowing softly through paper doors and windows. A vase of freshly cut flowers stood in an alcove behind her.

Lechasseur stepped out of the shadows and stood before her. 'Hello, Emily.'

Her skin crawled and her hackles went up. The fear was returning. The park, the fortune-teller, memory was returning.

'Emily. I want you to know, I've found some friends. Don't be scared. They don't want to hurt you.'

'You're not Honoré,' she said with a great, shuddering breath, suddenly sensing the difference in the figure before her. 'Stay away from me.'

'Please don't worry. My friends just want to ask you a few questions.' The familiar face twisted itself into a smile – but something else glittered in the eyes. 'That's all.'

Squatting, twisting and grabbing the vase of flowers in the alcove, in one adrenalin-rushed movement, Emily flung the vase into the figure's face.

She wrenched open the nearest sliding paper door, and ran out into the corridor. There were old, time-faded murals on every wall. An angry bellow sounded from the room behind her, and, seemingly in response, there came the sound of swift footfalls from somewhere else in the building; quiet but concentrated activity.

Emily hesitated at the end of the corridor and turned to look behind her.

Shadows stirred. A group of figures clad entirely in black stood in the corridor. She could not make out their eyes. Something stepped from the room out of which Emily had just bolted.

It wasn't Honoré. It wasn't even remotely human.

Although it wore a kimono and sandals, its head was huge and shaggy, with a sleek and weasel-pointed snout. Round, dark eyes glinted with bestial ferocity. From the sleeves of its kimono protruded long, cruel blades, shaped like scythes. It turned to face the troop of shadows further back in the corridor, who warily unclipped objects that glinted like silver from their belts.

Emily turned the corner and ran.

'*Sore wa ikenai*,' Mochizuka was whispering. 'We cannot do this.'

'We just did, I'm afraid.'

Breaking into the park had been ludicrously easy. An open-mesh wire fence with three strands of barbed wire at the top was all that had been in their way. Hanayashiki at night was desperately sad; a jungle of angular shadows, blind plaster masks half-glimpsed in the moonlight.

In the dark, the haunted house was even more foreboding. The figure above its entrance – the Hakutaku – gleamed with an unhealthy phosphorescence, like the bellies of dead fish.

They climbed the bridge and hugged the shadows by the door. Lechasseur produced a length of wire from his pocket, with a hook at one end and a series of ridges in the middle. He bent down, and began to apply it to the antiquated lock.

The door surrendered without much of a struggle.

Inside, the paper doors facing them were crudely pierced with dozens of small holes, gaping like eyeless sockets. The panels slid smoothly open at Lechasseur's touch, and the two men moved cautiously through the interior, Lechasseur taking the lead. The air was close, and smelt of dust and paint. In the gloom, as Lechasseur's eyes adjusted, he was able to make out a narrow corridor stretching ahead of him, straw matting underfoot, paper walls held together by thin wooden struts glowing softly in the weak light.

'This place is maze,' Mochizuka whispered.

'I can see that.'

'But that is house design. You walk through maze, try to get out. Actors come.' Mochizuka gave an impersonation of a zombie lurching drunkenly, mouth open.

Lechasseur grinned. The reporter's hamming was too forced, too exaggerated.

It didn't serve to hide his fear at all.

'What are those lights on the walls?'

'*Chicken-deguchi*. Many exits. In case customer is really too scared.'

Moving slowly forward in the half-light, Lechasseur beckoned his companion to follow.

They moved on, step by muffled step, around the corner and into a series of narrow corridors, the paper windows glowing softly with light reflected from the exit signs. They felt their way with outstretched hands, fingers scraping across dry, dusty surfaces. The humidity of the trapped air was becoming uncomfortable. Through open doorways, things hunched in pools of darkness. The smooth plastic faces of the mannequins stared blindly at the intruders, hands, painted with fake blood, raised in gestures that might have been mute pleas for help.

'*Nan da, are!*'

Two children had appeared in front of them. One second there had been nothing to be seen, the next there was. Two girls, as identical as twin sisters, wearing snowy white kimonos with black sashes. Their long, shiny black hair hung down, covering most of their faces. Their eyes were blank and deathly white.

Mochizuka muttered something to himself, then stepped forward gingerly. The girls flickered out of existence without a sound.

'Hologram,' Mochizuka announced.

'What?'

'Hologram. Laser light. Must have left switched on by accident.'

Lechasseur shrugged and walked through the place where the twin girls had been.

The heat and darkness were intoxicating him. He could feel the sweat, as chilly as drops of melted ice, sliding down his temple and his upper cheek. He could feel his heartbeat stepping up its muffled pounding in his chest, like an engine with the handle broken. He could see his grandparents, pointing at the darkness outside their home. *You best be careful about the bayou, son. There are places on the edge, between here and there. Go too close and you'll fall across and never come back.*

Lechasseur motioned his colleague to stop: 'This is hopeless.'

'*Nani ga?*'

'Emily can't be in here.'

He lifted up his head and took in a deep, shuddering breath. Never thought about spirits much before, he mused. In a world where people were spending all their time and energy on blowing each other up, in a world where going from one meal to the next demanded all your ingenuity, there wasn't much time to think about spirits. Maybe that's where he'd been going wrong. Maybe he should be paying his respects, asking for help . . .

No, damn it. I can do this on my own.

He closed his eyes and concentrated, while Mochizuka peered nervously into the shadows.

There *was* something there.

Lechasseur opened his eyes again and pulled his colleague into a room off the main corridor, brushing aside the mouldering red lanterns that hung from the ceiling.

'Listen. Can you hear anything?'

'Ah . . . no.'

Lechasseur pressed his ear to a nearby wall, and then knelt down. 'It's coming from . . . below us.'

At first he had thought it was his imagination. Or perhaps his own body. The ringing of the blood in his head, the rumbling of the air in his guts, the panicked rhythm of his heart reminding him of his ludicrous fragility.

But no, this was outside of him, he was sure. A muffled, regular sound, like air-conditioning, but deeper, somehow . . . organic.

'Ah, yes,' said Mochizuka. 'It's like – almost like – '

'Like a heart beating.'

The two of them knelt down, pushing aside a waxwork figure clutching a gore-stained sword sticking out of its chest, and rolled up the straw matting covering the floor. Lechasseur produced his old army knife, poked it between the planks of wood beneath, and began to lever them upwards.

'Breaking into a place and doing damage is very regrettable,' Mochizuka commented.

The reporter had spoken very quietly, but even so, the sound of his voice in the still air was enough to make Lechasseur's heart pump even faster.

What's wrong with me? He thought. What is it about this place? The sweat was now trickling into his eyes, pooling on his palms and fingers, threatening to make him lose his grip on the knife. *Things out there in the bayou. They'll suck you down, son, get hold of your ankles and suck you down into the swamp. They'll crawl into your mouth and nose and eat you from the inside.* Lechasseur fought to keep his hands steady.

'*Mo ganbarranai,*' Mochizuka stammered.

'What?'

'Lechasseur-san . . . I cannot stand this.'

'It's okay. I know you got the fear; it's getting to me, too. But I think something's causing it deliberately.' The wood gave way with a crack, and Lechasseur pulled out a segment of planking. He shone the flashlight down into the hole. 'Well now . . . what do you make of that?'

Mochizuka shuffled closer to peer into the hole. He squinted down into the shadows, making out a mottled, smooth surface that seemed to be covered in wire or hair.

Or fur.

'*Nan de kore?* Is it – is it moving?'

'Yes. It's definitely moving. In time to that heartbeat thing we can hear.'

'So, is it – is it – ?'

'I think "alive" is the word you're looking for.'

Lechasseur looked up sharply. A flutter of movement had caught his eye. One of the red paper lanterns was swaying above Mochizuka's head as if caught in a breeze. Something glowed inside it, angry red light bleeding through the ripped paper.

But there was no breeze. The dusty air was close and still. Either something had knocked it, or . . .

'Move!' Lechasseur bellowed.

Wrapping his arms around the slender reporter, Lechasseur launched them both at the wall. The barrier of paper and thin wooden struts gave way under their weight, and they tumbled through into the room beyond, falling in a rain of splinters and ragged paper ribbons.

The room beyond the wall was lit up as a great gout of flame spewed from the lower mouth of the lantern.

The two men picked themselves up, and wordlessly leapt at the next wall. The barrier split with a great crash, and they found themselves back in one of the gloomy corridors.

'*Chicken-deguchi*,' Mochizuka panted. Lechasseur looked for the nearest glowing exit sign, and orientated himself toward it. He glanced behind; a handful of paper lanterns bobbed in the fetid air, tongues of flame licking out of ragged holes as they floated gently forward.

'Forget the exit,' said Lechasseur. 'Follow me.'

The two men charged forward, carving a straight line through the maze as they crashed through wall after wall. Mochizuka stumbled over a kimono-wearing dummy lying prone with its throat cut, and Lechasseur picked him up and almost threw him at the next wall.

Finally, they tumbled out through the tattered sliding entrance door, onto the platform by the bridge. They gratefully breathed in the damp, smoke-tinged night air.

Lechasseur motioned Mochizuka to keep walking. They crossed the bridge, stepping smartly away from the haunted house, making sure to keep to the shadows.

And then they stopped. Lechasseur had heard his name being called. He put an arm across Mochizuka's path to block him, head tilted towards the sound.

'Lechasseur. Over here!'

Emily was standing by the entrance to the rollercoaster.

She was still wearing the trouser suit from earlier in the day, but her trousers were stained with dirt, and her face looked pale and haggard. 'They had me, but I got away. This way! Quick!'

Lechasseur squinted at Emily. Something was ringing an alarm bell in his head. As he looked at her, something started to happen to her head. He turned and pushed Mochizuka in the opposite direction. Mochizuka looked back and exclaimed something in rapid Japanese.

Lechasseur glanced over his shoulder.

Emily's neck was stretching itself out to an impossible length, pushing the head upwards. Her jaw hinged itself downward, revealing sharp, gleaming teeth set in a yawning, red wetness. Sparks began to flash from her bulging eyes. The head surged towards them on its thick, flexible cable of neck, tongue flicking rapidly in and out like a snake's. Between her hands, a ball of blue fire began to glow, growing larger as Lechasseur stared. Then he and Mochizuka turned and ran for the front gate.

They wasted no time in hoisting themselves over the metal bars and dropping down on to the other side. 'The car,' Lechasseur gasped. The keys were already in Mochizuka's hand.

As they ran into the night, an unearthly howl went up from within the shadowed amusement park, and the night was lit up briefly by blue lightning.

6: JUDAYU

Somewhere in the heart of Japan, the trees of an ancient forest hummed with life, their leaves rippling gently in the summer breeze. Cicadas buzzed like living dynamos. Birds chattered unceasingly to each other from the treetops. A woman, slim and with long dark hair, dressed in a city-smart trouser suit, was walking along a narrow dirt track.

As she walked, Emily looked around her, searching for any signs of civilization. In the ditch by the side of the track, the duckweed was so thick and voluptuous that the water could hardly be seen. Across the ditch, the blackened gold stems of the bamboo grove were so tightly pressed together that passage through them seemed impossible. The violent white petals of hollyhocks flashed like butterfly wings among the grass.

The only sign of life so far had come from a worn milestone, half-covered in lichen, that had indicated names and places that told her nothing.

She was still trying to make sense of what she had seen when she had woken. She had escaped through a courtyard, and hidden in a thick clump of bushes. The building in which she had found herself was some kind of shrine, but old, so old, and the decay of long disuse hung everywhere in the air. She had seen a struggling knot of men in black burst from the shrine entrance, dragging – *something* – with them, the thing lashed with ropes that the men used to control its movements.

But her mind could not register what the thing had been. It had been protean, shapeless, blurred in its wasted efforts to escape, moving so swiftly that it could not be seen.

And she still could not accept that the soldiers had been wearing blindfolds.

She trudged onward, wondering if there was anything in this forest that would prove to be edible. In front of her, she noticed wisps of smoke curling above the trees. Muttering a half-remembered prayer, she hurried on. As the dirt track curved slightly, a clearing in the distance came into view, and Emily stopped as a flash of movement caught her eye.

Two figures were walking along the dirt track in her direction. Hiding and shying away from people wasn't going to get her anywhere, so she strode towards them, waving her arms to signal.

They became aware of her, and both figures stopped and visibly flinched in surprise. As she got closer, Emily could see them more clearly; they were wearing old-fashioned tunics and breeches. And there was something decidedly odd about their hair; they wore it bunched up right on top of their heads in a topknot.

This wasn't looking too good. Oh well, she thought, in for a penny, in for a pound.

'Excuse me,' she called. 'I've had an accident, and I'm lost. Could you tell me where I am?'

The two men hurriedly conferred with each other – with more than a hint of panic, she thought. At length, one of them stepped forward, his hand placed upon something in his belt.

'What kind of trick is this?' he called. 'Are you mad, or are you some kind of demon?'

I thought so, Emily reflected. This isn't the twenty-first century any more. Not even the twentieth. I'll be lucky if it's the nineteenth.

The man in front glanced back at his comrade, and then pulled from his belt a long, curved sword, which gleamed in the sunlight.

'You know that the Shogunate has forbidden the foreign barbarians to travel inland!' he yelled. 'You are either a barbarian spy, or an evil spirit wearing the form of a barbarian!'

'She is a spirit sent to entrance us with her comely aspect,' his comrade replied. 'Let us find out if spirits bleed.'

'She is a spy, I say. The Daimyo will reward us greatly when we drag her corpse to the castle and hang it up for display.'

'After we strip those jewels from her neck, of course. Cut her where she stands!'

Emily didn't waste any more time on explanations. She turned and ran, her feet digging into the soft earth for traction, heading for the ditch.

Just as she was about to throw herself into the duckweed, a blur of movement and a howl of pain made her pause and turn.

The lead samurai's sword was now in the dirt, and he was clenching his hand in pain. The other was staring stupidly at an arrow that was still quivering, embedded in a sycamore tree just behind him.

Another figure now bolted out from the trees, legs scissoring as he held up the skirts of his kimono to increase his speed. As he reached the dirt track, he suddenly fell to his knees, sliding to a stop in front of the two samurai.

'My name is Judayu Kokichi!' the newcomer barked, his back to Emily. 'My pardon, young sirs. It is my duty to tell you that the jurisdiction of your Lord does not extend to this village. You have no right to shed blood here, of any animal or human. I beg you to sheath your swords, and depart in peace.'

Emily watched, her breath rasping in her ears, ready to break for the forest at the first sign of things not going her way.

The leading samurai screeched in rage, and raised his sword above his head. 'I will not honour a rogue such as you with my name, old man!'

Violence was a thing that still sickened Emily. London fist fights were bad enough, but angry men waving long, sharp-pointed objects was something she had never wished to be party to. She turned away, but the awful immediacy of the moment made her keep the newcomer in her peripheral vision, as he dealt with the two samurai.

She needn't have felt so squeamish. The fight was over before it began. Judayu moved like the forest dragonflies, his body twisting in a light-footed dance along the path, his sword criss-crossing the air to attack and parry.

He left the two men unarmed and semi-conscious, their only injuries bruised wrists and bleeding fingers where their swords had been swept from their grasp. He then turned towards Emily, sheathing his sword in one swift, fluid motion. Now she could see his face, she could see he was a lot older than she had thought, his lean, weather-browned face that of a man of maybe forty or more. His hair, unlike that of Emily's two attackers, was not restrained by a topknot, and fell upon his shoulders and over his face in long tresses. His kimono was old, and faded in parts, but with intricate floral patterns still visible across the front.

'It is not safe for you to be here,' he said, unsmilingly.

'Erm, I'd sort of guessed that. It's true, though . . . I *am* a traveller who's got lost.' She stopped talking, giving him a charming, helpless smile that made her feel her own helplessness even more. 'You see, I don't have anywhere to go!'

Judayu stared at her in silence. His gaze was so intense that she began to blush, to look around at the trees, anything to get away from those browny-black eyes.

Finally, he turned away from her and started walking. 'Follow me,' he called.

They walked together in silence, Judayu always at least half a dozen steps in front of Emily, along the dirt track.

They walked for almost an hour, during which time Emily's throat grew dryer and dryer. At last, their path took them to the lower dip of a valley, with the village that Judayu had mentioned spread out before them.

Emily surveyed the landscape, which consisted mainly of scores of rice-fields receding into the trees of the forest that encircled them. The water in the fields glowed in the summer sunlight like rows of mirrors for the face of Heaven, and above the fields the air shimmered with swarms of green and silver dragonflies, swooping through the haze on translucent wings. The sky was an unbroken mother-of-pearl.

Workers stood knee-deep in the water, straw hats or thin silk cloths covering their heads. They slowly unfolded themselves like herons as Judayu and his unexpected guest approached. There were children among them, leaping to catch the dragonflies with long bamboo brooms.

Judayu led Emily around the edge of the village, deliberately, she thought, sparing her the indignity of being the object of close observation. The huts were all dark, wooden, box-like constructions, with sack-like curtains, daubed with broad splashes of ink, covering the windows. Bundles of pampas grass were tied in place above the doors. Emily followed Judayu to what he indicated was his hut, and he led her inside.

'This is a very poor residence,' he said, courteously, 'but I will offer you what I can.'

Emily stepped out of the sunlight into the cool, earth-smelling gloom. The small, narrow hut was divided into two sections by a long bamboo screen at the back. Near the entrance, to her left, lay an open hearth, a huge iron kettle above it, suspended from a chain. On the other side of the hut was an undecorated, shadowed alcove with a pile of blankets. Behind her, a curious, arrow-like charm hung above the door.

Judayu spread out a coarse blanket for her to sit on. 'I'd like to thank you for helping me out, back there,' Emily began, brightly. 'You saved my life.'

'It is extremely dangerous to wander the woods and the back lanes. All kinds or rogues lurk along the perimeter, just looking to attack and rob the unwary.' He turned to face her, his long face frowning and quizzical. 'So, permit me to ask what an outsider is doing a place such as this, and why you speak such natural Japanese. Were you sent by the Dutch? Or the Portuguese? To gather news on the state of the conflict?'

'No, really, what I told you was true. I'm – I'm British. I really am a traveller who got lost, I, er, I work for the Admiral. My name is Emily. Can you fill me in a little on what's going on around here? I mean, what was that conflict you mentioned?'

Judayu passed her a bowl of cold, bitter tea, and sipped from his own thoughtfully. 'I don't know much about the ways of the Portuguese,' he pondered, 'but I don't think they are the kind of people to let a woman wander around unprotected. That would be a very poor way of spying. So you may be telling the truth.'

He took the lid off the kettle and sniffed the thin fish broth that still remained within. Adding handfuls of radish, burdock root and soy, he lit a fire in the heart beneath the pot.

'Know you, then,' he said, leaning forward and staring at Emily intently, 'that this village is coveted by two fiefdoms. One belongs to Lord Kaishun, and the other to Lord Nazaeyamon. We straddle the territory of both. We nominally belong to Lord Nazaeyamon, but are still plagued by occasional raiding parties from Lord Kaishun.'

'I suppose these two Lords aren't too keen on each other, then?'

'There have been land disputes and breaches of etiquette for as long as I can remember. But this is the way of things. It is normal for Daimyo to behave in this fashion, for do they not have the power to decide life or death, with but a word or a gesture? No, this is not the cause of the sorrow here. This is not our . . . curse.'

Judayu lapsed into silence for a moment, and Emily thought she'd better prompt him. 'Does this have anything to do with spirits?'

'Spirits, you say?'

'The spirits of beasts. Beasts that walk like men. Well, actually, women.'

Judayu started, and gazed at Emily with a new interest. 'The Kitsune. The attendants of Inari-sama. It does indeed.'

'So, are these Kitsune attacking the village, then?' Emily thought about what Mochizuka had told them in Tokyo, and then decided to try to put the picture together. 'Have there been stories of people disappearing? Of people dying in strange . . . circumstances?'

Judayu stood up abruptly, turning back toward the fireplace.

'Not before Lord Nazaeyamon declared war upon them.'

He stared moodily at the glowing charcoal logs, as if seeing visions in the embers. 'That one had always been slightly apart from the world. He was a delicate, sickly child. Spent his early days reading the ancient scrolls, and devoted far more attention to the occult that is healthy. But he was the only male child of the Daimyo, and was of a fit age to succeed when his father died.'

Judayu took a deep, shuddering breath. 'He seemed not such a disaster at first. Capricious and greedy, yes, but these things could be dealt with. But over the past years, he has grown more and more wilful. Something is disordered in his brain. Perhaps you know, it is customary for Daimyos to enter the ranks of the Gods, after they die. Their remains are placed in the shrines, and they join the ranks of their honourable ancestors in watching over us. But Lord Nazaeyamon has gone further than that. He has declared himself to be a *living* God. He considers himself to have power over the invisible world, the passage of the sun and moon, the destiny of men's souls. He has constructed a shrine to himself, within his castle. And, as he has declared himself a God, he will not countenance any other spirit trespassing on his land. And so he has declared war upon the Kitsune.'

'So, these fox-things, you know they're real? You're saying they live somewhere in the forest?'

Judayu turned to her with a little smile. 'Young foolish one, everyone knows that the Kitsune are *real*. Every animal, every tree and every lake, every mountain has a God within it. If it were not so, we would not devote offerings to them at the Festival. The Kitsune have been known since beyond living memory. But now Lord Nazaeyamon's campaign has sorely depleted their ranks. The shrine to Inari-sama has been boarded up; it was only the pleas of the Daimyo's mother that stopped him from burning it to the ground.'

'I think I'm beginning to see what's going on,' Emily said, slowly. 'But what exactly are you doing here? I mean, you don't look like a farmer, Judayu. And you certainly don't fight like one.'

Judayu stared broodingly into his tea. 'It was the Kitsune that led to my downfall,' he sighed. 'Indirectly.'

'You were a samurai, weren't you?'

'Yes.'

'And one of the best?'

Judayu laughed. 'How many of "the best" have you seen, young lady?'

'I take your point.'

Judayu ladled out fish soup into two bowls, and handled one to her with a cup of rice. Emily accepted it gracefully.

'Mistress Emily, I was once a retainer to the Lord Nazaeyamon. My shame began when my young daughter, a girl well-loved by the court, began to sicken and not heal. Priests treated her. Physicians treated her. And then her bouts of illness and abnormal behaviour were suspected to be signs of fox-enchantment.

'Several exorcisms were conducted, to no effect. Lord Nazaeyamon ruled that my daughter – my real daughter – had been killed by a fox who had taken her shape to spy on the castle. She was executed.'

Emily paused in her eating, her appetite suddenly gone.

'And then, weeks after, one of the sons of another retainer confessed to a court priest. My daughter had not been possessed. She had been pregnant. They had been lovers for a considerable time, but because there were talks to marry my daughter to the son of a higher-ranking official, they had been unable to say anything.'

Judayu put down his bowls. 'I, along with the boy and his father, were ordered to cut off our top-knots and become *ronin* – masterless samurai.'

'Why?'

'Because our tragedy was compounded by the shame of an inappropriate relationship.'

Emily blinked.

'And so I retired, to the edge of the village, which belongs neither to one Lord nor to the other. It seemed fitting. I lead a simple life, I offer my services to the villagers when they need them. It is enough.'

'Judayu, I don't know much about Japan, especially not in this day and age, but why doesn't someone do something about Nazaeyamon? A little judicious assassination, for example?'

Judayu snorted with laughter, and shook his head wearily. 'There would be war. Lord Kaishun would invade the territory, and the villages would be at the whim of his samurai. Who knows what would befall the people? At least, at the moment, Lord Nazaeyamon leaves the common folk alone. He is more concerned . . . with the foxes.'

Judayu took a glowing sprig of wood from the hearth, and lit a candle. The dark jumped into relief around them, a solid, physical thing. *These people live with the spirits*, Emily told herself. *There is no telling where this world ends and the next world begins.*

'Midsummer nights are when the dead come back to visit us,' he pronounced. 'Sometimes, I feel that one day there shall be no-one living to greet them.'

7: THE KITSUNE

The fish regarded Lechasseur with cold, dead eyes. Lechasseur stared back.

His breakfast in the Hotel Kent was so far untouched. He sat, possibilities racing through his mind, as he rejected one idea after another, his lips twitching in time with his thoughts.

Emily was gone. And if she didn't come back, he was stuck here. But that concern paled beside the thought of what those . . . *things* might have done to her.

He looked up as a figure approached his table; Mochizuka, in another smart-looking suit, his face, as always, perfectly-composed, but dark, telltale pools of shadow under his eyes.

'*Ohio gozaimasu*, Lechasseur-san. How are you today?'

'Things could be a whole lot better. How about you?'

'I am exhausted.' The reporter bowed briefly and flopped onto the seat opposite. He glanced at the selection of food spread over the table: a whole grilled fish, its eyes bulging and milky; a radish salad shot through with tiny, desiccated prawns; a dish on the other side containing a slimy, stringy oil.

'Did you get through to Kyoto?'

'*Hai*. Er – yes. I have also spoke to manager, and he agree. We will video-conference at nine-thirty.'

Lechasseur looked up at the dining room clock. Ten minutes away.

'Lechasseur-san, have you looked at television today?'

'No. Should I?'

Mochizuka paused, for a second. His face was dazed, his lips slack. Lechasseur caught a momentary glimpse of the man's time-worm, and shuddered. Whatever was coming, was nearly with them.

'I think for you should see something.'

The hotel manager showed them to the lounge, where there were already a large number of guests. Businessmen on their own, a handful of couples, two or three families with babies in complicated-looking carriages. They whispered tensely amongst themselves, gazes flicking back and forth from their companions in the room to the high-resolution flat-screen television placed along the back wall.

'They have shown this all morning,' Mochizuka informed Lechasseur. 'On every channel. Was taken by a traffic patrol helicopter TV crew.'

Helicopter. Lechasseur's mind filed the word away for future reference. On screen, the presenter's desk-bound image suddenly disappeared, to be replaced by an ariel view of the city. It was definitely Tokyo, but he could not identify the buildings. The camera swooped and shook as the aircraft it was in descended towards the nearest multi-story building.

There was a woman on the roof.

The camera swung in closer. She was crouching down on the roof, hands and knees resting on the asphalt. Her hair was up in a fashion that reminded Lechasseur of the revellers at the Festival in Kyoto, and she was wearing a formal kimono. He knew that if the camera could get in close enough, they would be able to see the three ragged claw-marks, courtesy of Hide and Chic. The woman stared back at the approaching camera, head twisted back over her shoulder.

She moved. Crawling on all fours, at unexpected and obscene speed. Towards the edge of the roof –

– and crawled right over, without stopping. There was a strangled gasp from all inside the dining room.

The camera plunged lower, swinging around the side of the building, and even Lechasseur flinched. The screen froze on that moment, the film stopped to capture the moment in time, to play and replay, back and forth.

The woman was clinging to the side of the building, on all fours, arms and legs spread in a posture that reminded him of geckos scaling walls in the bayou. Her head twisted back, she stared into the camera with implacable hatred.

And then the film resumed its motion, and she scuttled down the side of the building, head downward. The dining room started buzzing with conversation, like a disturbed hive. The women with children pushed them quickly out of the room, their faces pale.

'Listen,' Lechasseur turned to the reporter. 'Something's got to be done soon. Whatever's haunting this city, it's getting bolder and bolder. Like it's ready to make a move. What time is it?'

'Past nine-thirty.'

'Then let's talk to the priest.'

The hotel manager had reserved the conference room for the two of them, and Lechasseur found himself facing another TV screen, this time with a camera next to it. The screen was filled with the face of Akihira Noguchi, peering owlishly at them through his thick eyeglasses.

'Lechasseur-san, *ohio gozaimasu*. How is your stay?'

'Well it's . . . eventful. Thank you for agreeing to our request at such short notice, Noguchi-san. We need your advice. What do you know about foxes?'

'Foxes?'

'Yes. The shrines of the Fox-Goddess, Inari-sama.'

There was a pause. The old man's face changed visibly as he muttered something in Japanese.

'What was that?'

'*Tatari*. They are cursed.'

Lechasseur waited for the priest to continue. He did not.

'Noguchi-san, I haven't got time to explain, but I think what's happening in Tokyo is something to do with those shrines. Could you be a little more . . . specific?'

The priest took a deep breath. 'We Japanese take the Kitsune – the fox-spirits – very seriously. There are shrines to Inari-sama all over Japan. There are so many stories, from ancient times, when humans lived side by side with the spirits of nature.'

'What do these stories say?'

'The Kitsune are trickster-spirits. Sometimes a force for good, some-times for evil, or what humans would consider evil. In the old folk stories, they would mostly help people, but sometimes they would trick people . . .

or avenge themselves if they had been wrongly treated.'

'Would they trick or deceive people for sport?'

'No. Not exactly. They are bound by a strict set of codes of honour, just like our society is. They appear to confuse people and be contra-dictory, but amongst themselves, they are consistent in their behaviour.'

'What powers do they have?'

'They can appear in any shape they wish. They can wear the form of a beautiful woman, or the most frightening ghoul. They can entrance the human mind, and fill it with the most fantastic dreams and illusions. There is another story – recorded in the *Kojiki*, the Japanese creation myths – that tells of the *Kurokabe*. The Black Wall. It is a gateway to the spirit world, through which the Kitsune travel.'

Lechasseur clicked his tongue, lost in thought.

'Let's say, for the purpose of argument,' he continued, 'that these foxes, these Kitsune, appeared in modern Tokyo. That they came back. Do you think it likely that they would . . . get up to their old tricks? Hunt people? Kill them?'

'Lechasseur-san, the Kitsune *do not* kill in cold blood. And they do not hunt humans for sport. One notable thing about the stories is their sense of justice. If the Kitsune are wronged, they will retaliate, but they are not needlessly cruel. Remember; Inari-sama is also the Goddess of rice and harvests. They can be cruel, yes, but they can be charitable. Do you know there are no fox legends on the island of Shikoku?'

'Why's that?'

'Because there are no foxes on Shikoku.'

Lechasseur snorted with mirthless laughter. 'Noguchi-san . . . I don't really have the *time* . . .'

'*Gomen nasai*, Lechasseur-san. Please forgive an old fool. But the story of how the foxes left Shikoku is interesting. The story tells us that a fox-spirit impersonated the wife of a nobleman to confuse the nobles and to provide entertainment for the Kitsune themselves. When the woman's husband discovered the deception, he ordered that every fox on the island should be slain.

'But the next day, the fox-spirits arrived, as a group, to apologise and ask for the animals to be spared. At length, the nobles and the Kitsune came an agreement. You see, they *negotiated*. There was a time when harmony was reached between man and spirits, although this seems impossible now. And so, according to their vow, the Kitsune sailed away from Shikoku, to seek a new home.'

Lechasseur sat back, trying to digest all the new information. 'Noguchi-san, this is helpful. Most helpful.'

'Have you thought more about the rabbit? My father's riddle?' Noguchi suddenly asked. 'If it could speak, what would it say?'

Lechasseur frowned. 'It would probably say that it would rather be a fox.'

Emily dreamed.

It was a long, confusing dream, and quite different from her usual night-terrors. She was being pursued through the woods. No matter how fast she tried to run, she never seemed to make any headway. Her legs felt incredibly heavy, like she was swimming in molasses.

The thing that was chasing her howled. She plunged onward through mist and leaf-mould, stumbling past trunk-like stems of bamboo, red stains splashed upon the green. Above her, a storm of crows croaked as they took flight in panic. Leaving the wood. Forsaking Emily and whatever was hunting her.

The mulchy forest floor giving way beneath her, Emily pitched forward, and jerked awake with a cry.

It was broad daylight, motes of dust sparkling in the damp, close air of the hut. Emily was lying on bare earth, in clothes that were gritty with sweat, the sack-like blanket twisted around her.

The noise that had awoken her repeated itself. A man's voice, shouting, from outside. Judayu, at the window, let the curtain fall back into place as he looked down at Emily. 'You will stay here.' Then he was through the door, marching outside. Emily scrambled to the window, lifting her head up cautiously to see outside.

There were six horses and their riders outside, and Judayu was striding out to face them. They were not at all like the two men who had accosted her on the road the day before. They wore breastplates of overlapping scales of metal, held together with knotted metal cords. Their arms and legs were fitted with supple-looking greaves and gauntlets, short boots with studded soles resting in the stirrups. On their heads they wore steel helmets with visors, wings protecting the sides of the face, and the crest of an insect resembling a dragonfly painted on the front.

But the oddest thing was, that they all had thick scarves of green material wrapped around their eyes. Emily peered hard, to make sure that she wasn't mistaken. She wasn't. Each of the riders – except for two who stayed far back, almost at the place where the village huts began – had a thick blindfold with the same dragonfly crest covering his eyes.

The rider in front, who was obviously a captain of the guard or someone of similar rank, called imperiously to Judayu.

'So, you are the once-famous Judayu Kokichi. You know, the men still laugh about you and your misfortunes over a few cups of rice wine. But I never expected to meet you in person. It is very stupid of you to upset the Daimyo a second time, you know.'

'I am indeed a stupid old man. Perhaps if I cut off your head and put it on my shoulders next to mine, I would be smarter. Now state your business plainly and then be gone.'

'Our business, plainly, is that we have been informed that you are harbouring a foreigner. Your village is well known for being tardy in offering taxes to the Daimyo. Now, it seems, you are sheltering an outsider. This will not be received very well, I assure you.'

In the shadowed interior of the hut, Emily sucked in her breath. The villagers, she thought.

'The girl is a traveller, who was lost in the forest,' Judayu barked. 'How dare you commit such acts of rudeness in the name of the Daimyo!'

'Rudeness? Don't speak to me of etiquette, old man. I have broken no etiquette, here, because you are beneath significance.' He grinned humourlessly at the *ronin*, and then sat up proudly in his saddle. 'Now surrender the girl to us, or I'll cut you in half and burn down your hovel to get at her!'

'There'll be no need for that,' Emily called. All heads turned to where the voice had come from. Emily had left the hut and walked out into plain view. Judayu stared at her, furiously. 'I'll come with you,' she said to the messenger.

'Mistress Emily,' Judayu muttered softly.

'This is not your fault,' Emily told him, as sternly as she could, trying to conceal the trembling in her limbs. 'This is a decision that *I* am making. Do not try to follow me, Judayu.'

The *ronin* bowed his head once. 'That is a promise I cannot make, Mistress Emily.'

The captain turned his head away, and beckoned to the blindfolded men behind him. Four of them dismounted, and stood there for a second, cocking their heads in a curious way, like dogs. Then they started to walk slowly, but steadily, towards Emily. All of them were connected by a length of rope held in their hands, and they fanned out as they walked towards Emily, as if they were spiders and Emily the cowering fly before them.

Of course, she thought, as they got closer. These fox things can hypnotise people. Maybe if you can't see them, it doesn't work. That's why these men are working blind.

Emily stayed where she was as the soldiers finally reached her. Working by touch, they began to wind the rope around her, pinioning her arms to her sides.

After they had securely bound her, two of them slipped their hands into her pockets. Emily shuddered, but their faces betrayed no emotion, no gloating excitement, as they extracted the few possessions that she had brought with her. The mobile phone and the wristwatch were the source of brief but intense conversation between the group captain and Emily's guards. The phone was handed to the captain, who flipped it open and shut several times. He started visibly as the phone gave out its little musical chime when the cover was opened.

Eventually, Emily was put up on a horse behind one of the riders – who, mercifully, wasn't blindfolded. As the horse trotted away, she craned her neck to see Judayu behind her, motionless at the door of his hut.

There was no flicker of emotion upon his face as he watched the party leave.

Lechasseur paced the hotel room restlessly while he waited for Mochizuka to return from the car with what he'd asked him to fetch.

Something is in the streets, he thought. Something has broken out; it's slipped its leash and is now loose. The fetid air that spewed out from the city's air-conditioned buildings was like ragged breath from its throat. The darkness that oozed from among the trees in the city parks was shot through with the cold, hard glinting of its eyes.

Mochizuka stepped through the door, slipping off his shoes and holding out what he'd brought. The gifts from the fashion show; the two jackets and the dress with which they had been presented by Ikari's model.

Lechasseur gingerly took the three items. He sat down on the bed, produced a cheap artist's cutting knife that he'd bought in the hotel convenience store, and eased the blade into the first jacket's inner lining.

'*Nan de koto!* Hey, what you doing? This is Hide and Chic original!'

'I'm making a few alterations.'

Teasing the lining away from the stitching, while Mochizuka winced at the ripping sounds, Lechasseur held the jacket up to the light. 'Well, will you look at that.'

They looked.

Inside the jacket was a thin layer of dark, furry pelt, its dun colour speckled with patches of red and white. It seemed to change colour as they looked at it, shimmering like the tonic mohair of the jacket's exterior, and, as Lechasseur looked closely, he could see that the suggestion of movement was not an illusion.

It was pulsating slightly in the room's dry air.

'This is same as we found under floor of haunted house?'

'Yes. I'm pretty sure it's the same stuff we saw last night.'

'So why it's in jacket?'

'I don't know.'

Lechasseur carefully slit open the linings of the other two gifts, quickly confirming that they also contained the same furry, pulsating material. He gently folded up the garments and laid them on the bed beside him. Suddenly very tired, he bent forward and put his head in his hands.

They must be putting that stuff in all their clothes, he thought. People are fighting to get their hands on these brands, and this is what's in them. Poison. Ikari has contaminated this city. This place was schizoid to begin with, but now it's been tipped over the edge.

Lechasseur sighed, lifted up his head. He felt in his pocket for the lucky rabbit's foot charm, pulled it out, held it between his hands and stared at it.

'Hey, buddy.' Mochizuka's voice had assumed a clumsy American twang. 'What's matter?'

'Just thinking about the guy who used to own this.'

'Very good friend, *ne?*'

'Actually, I hardly knew him.' Lechasseur blinked. 'You know, if we can't really understand other people, I don't think we've got much of a chance of figuring out these things running around Tokyo.'

He put down the charm, tried to rub the fatigue from his eyes. 'And if the rabbit could speak, what would it say?'

'Ah, that what priest say to you. *Naruhodo*. I used to have a rabbit when I was children. Very, very cute, *honto-ni*. To tell you the truth, I wanted to be rabbit.'

'Is that so.'

'*Un*. But now, I realize that is too hard. Maybe I don't like being rabbit. Rabbit has to live outside and eat the grass. Me, I am rabbit, I don't want eat the grass. I want eat some – *honto-ni, oishii mono*. Like really nice sushi.'

Lechasseur started to giggle. Then, before he could contain himself, he burst out laughing. He looked sideways at Mochizuka, and tried to remember the last time he had laughed.

'You know, Mochizuka-san, you're okay.'

'Really? *Arigato*!'

Lechasseur stood up. 'Come on.'

'Ah, where are we going?'

'Back to Asakusa.'

Mochizuka's enthusiasm disappeared like a switch had been thrown. '*Mata? Uso, darro . . .*'

Although he couldn't understand the language, Lechasseur appreciated the sentiment. ''Fraid so. Whatever this stuff is, there's got to be a reason why there's so much of it under the floor of a haunted house. Maybe Ikari or whoever will come back for it. So let's go and keep an eye on the place . . . and bring that jacket with you, put it back in the car.'

8: LORD NAZAEYAMON

It took the best part of a day for Emily and her armed escort to travel on horseback to their destination. Although they stopped frequently to rest and to stretch their legs, Emily was starting to think that she wouldn't be able walk on solid ground ever again.

Their eventual destination was set among gentle hills, at the end of a long avenue lined with cryptomeria. A set of massive wooden gates stood before them. The air was fragrant with the scent of the trees and nearby water.

The captain called out to unseen ears, and the gates began to swing open. Grooms in strange uniforms with horizontal stripes, that made Emily think of pictures of Victorian bathing costumes, rushed out to guide the horses through the gates and to help the riders dismount. Gatekeepers armed with bows and halberds saluted them as they passed.

She found herself in the open yard of a large complex of buildings, some of which she could identify as stables, storehouses and plain wooden outbuildings that could conceivably be lodgings for servants. There were also courtyards, gardens, and, in front of her, a huge building with a thick, tiled roof shining silver and brown. This, then, was the stronghold of the Daimyo. At each corner of the complex stood a watchtower, a shadowy figure moving around within it.

Emily was carried to a chamber, where she was laid on another earthen floor, this time pitted and stained by things she didn't want to speculate about.

The blindfolded guards cut her bonds by touch alone, and retreated backwards, closing the windowless door. She listened to the keys rattle in the lock as she rubbed her cramped limbs. Chin up, Emily, she thought. They brought you here for a purpose. If they wanted to kill you, they would have just run you through with one of their fancy swords.

Across the room, something stirred.

As her eyes adjusted to the gloom, she could see that the irregular bump in the floor was actually a blanket. With someone underneath it.

'Hello?' she whispered, nervously. 'My name is Emily Blandish. It's all right, I'm not a spirit or a devil.' Stupid, she thought; that's exactly what they'd expect a devil to say.

The only reply was an incomprehensible moan.

She shuffled over to the blanket. 'Are you hurt?' she asked, softly. 'Can I help?' She thought of torture, of what a Japanese tyrant was capable of doing in such an age. Her hand reached out and gently pulled back the blanket.

She froze where she was, mouth open, looking down at her fellow prisoner, her shock mixed with an undeniable sense of wonder.

The head underneath the blanket lolled with its mouth open. No, not mouth, *jaws* – full of curved, pointed teeth, a long red tongue out and slavering as the creature panted in misery. Emily could feel the reality of its hot breath upon her hand. Black eyes blinked at her from matted, reddish-brown fur, and a pointed snout protruded below a narrow, sloping forehead.

A fox. A fox-spirit.

Despite her feelings of fear and disgust, Emily could see that the creature was hurt. The sleeve of the thing's kimono was clotted with dried, reddish stains. At least the blood's the same colour, she thought. As she gingerly touched its hand, the creature flinched, but did not pull away.

Well, I can't just sit here while someone is in pain, she thought; and that goes for animals and spirits as well as people. She pulled the blanket away completely, gingerly checking the body beneath the kimono. She had no idea what was normal for a fox that dressed like a human woman, but the pulse seemed rapid and weak, and moving the right wrist caused the thing to give out a heartbreaking whimper, as if there was a fracture beneath the skin. Tearing the thin blanket in half, she wrapped it around the creature's forearm to secure it against the left shoulder, tying the makeshift sling in a reef knot.

Thank you, someone said in her head.

Emily knew that she was never really hearing people speak her own language; when she had listened to Mochizuka and his colleagues back in Tokyo, something in her mind had boiled down the stew of words and left her with the essence, the meaning of what they were trying to say. A similar process seemed to work the other way round. She would think what she wanted to say, and the appropriate language would somehow be heard by the other party. But this was different. Emily felt it more as a warm breath inside her head, the back of her skull tingling as words and concepts purred through her consciousness.

This was something beyond animal. And truly beyond human.

I am Mamori, it said. *Why are you here? You are not Kitsune. Why do the bold ones trap one of their own?*

'That's because I am not one of these people. I am not like them.'

Emily shook her head, not just for emphasis but also from the bizarre sensation of having the inside of it licked by something like a cat's tongue.

'I think you'd better tell me as much as you can,' Emily said.

The creature lay still for long seconds, its head lolling back on the rough floor, and Emily thought for a moment that it might be asleep. But then it stirred, and the voice sounded once more in her head.

You do not have the scent of a village-dweller, it is true. You have the scent of sweat mixed with fire, oil, and fear. You have the smell of that place, where dreams are put in the box and pressed to death.

'You mean the city. The city in this land's future. Have you seen it?'

I have not seen it. But the clans have ridden through the Black Wall to make their new lair. But how do you travel? You have no Black Wall.

'I don't know what a Black Wall is.' Emily sat back, sighing in frustration and fatigue. 'And I don't know who, or what, you are.'

The fox lifted itself up on one arm, the kimono slipping back from its fur, turning its head to fix Emily with black, gleaming eyes. *We are Kitsune. We have lived, for ages, in this land. We have shared it with the bold ones. Our time is not the same as your time. We have not always been here, but we have made this our home. We have shared it with the other races, according to our laws and yours . . . until now.*

'What's happened to change things?'

The Kitsune let its head loll back on the filthy ground, exhausted. *War*, it said, simply.

The guards came for Emily at sundown.

They came, feeling their way with the dragonfly symbol blindfolds pulled down over their eyes, to spin webs of rope around her body once again. Emily had accepted it as inevitable. What did dismay her, however, was that they also bound the injured Mamori, and forced her – not it, she thought – to stumble along beside her. They were obviously being taken to the same destination.

In the main building at the heart of the complex, they were both led down a series of corridors with straw matting floors and delicate hanging scrolls upon the paper walls. At length, they stopped in front of a gilded screen painted with a snarling tiger's face. The screen then slid smoothly aside, admitting them to a large antechamber. At the back of the room, the windows were open, revealing the fading glories of the sunset, and throwing into shadow an angular figure seated behind a low table. Standing in alcoves around the room were a number of bulky, metallic objects. Emily considered that, with her luck, they were probably instruments of torture. The guards forced the prisoners into a kneeling position in front of the table.

After a contemplative pause, a silky voice broke the silence.

'My messengers were not lying,' it said. 'As a woman, you wear a handsome shape. It will be a pleasure to compose a haiku on your beauty, after your death.'

'I appreciate that,' Emily replied.

The figure rose slowly, the light falling upon his features as he rose to his feet.

He was a slender, youngish man, his face almost womanly, with high cheekbones and delicate features. He was wrapped in a gorgeous, long-sleeved kimono, his legs hidden by full-trousered pantaloons of stiff yellow silk. A conical hat of black, lacquered fabric was held snugly to his head by a dark chinstrap.

'First foxes, and now foreigners,' he said. 'You were part of a raiding party, I presume? And became separated from your superiors?'

'You're making a mistake,' Emily told him, trying to put some authority into her voice. 'I am a British citizen, and I – I was shipwrecked.'

He chuckled softly. 'Shipwrecked? Are you aware how far we are from the sea, Lady Barbarian?'

The air was filled with the rustling of silk as the man glided towards her, the pantaloons hiding his feet and making the movement seem unearthly.

'I strongly advise you to show at least some consideration for my intelligence,' he said quietly, pushing his face close to Emily's. 'I am Lord Nazaeyamon. We are well equipped to deal with your kind, and will not tolerate disrespect. Are you aware how many I have had executed for showing disrespect?'

Emily's mouth twisted unconsciously into a grimace. 'I have no idea.'

The Daimyo lifted his gaze from Emily to stare into the middle distance, a whimsical smile on his lips.

'Neither have I,' he said, quietly.

9: HAKUTAKU

'We know about the foxes, so maybe we also need to know something about the park,' Lechasseur was saying. 'Did you find out anything about that haunted house?'

'Yes, I think so.' Mochizuka swerved the car, as gently as he could, away from a young lady's wobbly progress on a bicycle. 'Haunted house always had a very bad memory. Since long time ago. Long time ago, it was zoo.'

Lechasseur raised an eyebrow. 'A zoo?'

'Yes, yes. Ah, no. Not exactly zoo, but like . . . *nan to yuu, ka na* . . . sideshow. Ever since Meiji era, they keep special animal, exotic animal, they keep them here. Bird of paradise, zebra, elephant, snake, spider . . . many animal. Then in Taisho era, big earthquake happen.'

'Which earthquake would that . . . oh, wait. The one in 1923, right?' Time travel had its advantages, and Lechasseur and Emily had spent many days in London's libraries researching significant world events of recent history.

'Yes, yes. Many damages in Tokyo. Big fire, and zoo burned down. All animals dead. Records say noise was unbearable. People cannot – could not stand the noise of animal screaming.'

Lechasseur rubbed his jaw. 'What happened after that?'

'It became unlucky place. Because people so scared, park's manager decide to make haunted house. Make money from – ah, I don't know.'

'Trade on its scary reputation?'

'Yes, yes. Hanayashiki grew up around original haunted house. But, even so, people still think it bad place. Some people feel things. Some people see things. Too scared.'

Parking the car a short distance from their destination, Lechasseur and Mochizuka made their way to the entrance on foot, only to find it cordoned off by police tape. Instead of the throng of parents and children that would normally be expected in the amusement park on a Sunday, there were only uniformed policemen to be seen within, with measuring tapes and evidence collection boxes spread out just beyond the entrance.

'Now just remember, last night had nothing to do with us,' Lechasseur cautioned needlessly.

The reporter presented his credentials at the gate, and the police officer looked long and hard at the card, then at Mochizuka, and then at Lechasseur. He gestured for them to follow him.

As they walked, Lechasseur studied the haunted house out of the corner of his eyes. Policemen stood in front of it with folded arms, glaring at the newcomers from beneath peaked caps. Then another, apparently more senior, police officer, a wiry man in a spotless uniform, emerged from the white roller-coaster building. Mochizuka bowed and presented his name-card once more. Lechasseur watched as the police officer studied it, then turned to Lechasseur, and – nostrils flaring – pushed his head closer and *sniffed* him.

Lechasseur blanched, and tugged at Mochizuka's arm.

'What's matter now?'

'Just turn around. Just apologise and let's head for the exit. Say we made a mistake.'

'Yes, I think a mistake would be a good way to put it,' came a familiar voice. 'This is your mistake.'

The voice came from their left; they both turned, the police officer moving with them. Ikari was standing next to the entrance of something called 'Space Shot'. She stood with her arms folded, relaxed, elegant in a Hide and Chic cocktail dress, her smile flawless but cold.

'Are these gentlemen with you?' Lechasseur jerked his thumb at the police officers.

'They are very convincing, don't you think? Almost as good as the models. Very similar, in fact. They don't have to say much, just walk around and frown a lot. That's enough to keep people happy.'

Casting a quick glance to the slack-jawed Mochizuka, Lechasseur stepped forward. 'My name is Honoré Lechasseur. Whom do I have the honour of addressing?'

'Ha! You learn quickly. Not like the rest of these thin-skinned bold ones.' She flicked her hair back. 'But you already know my name . . . I am Ikari, brood-mother of the White Claw Kitsune.'

Lechasseur frowned, trying to remember what Noguchi had told him. 'Well, Ikari, I'd say you've got some explaining to do.'

'Explaining? We have to explain ourselves? You are not called the bold ones for nothing. You are the ones who should have to explain. Explain how and why you have *spoiled everything*.'

As Ikari spoke, Lechasseur was becoming aware of something. He was listening to her speak in English, but there was a peculiar vibration underpinning her words – a vibration so subtle and so deep that it could have been inside his own head.

'We came here through the Black Wall,' she said. 'We came here to escape the persecution of an insane creature. A mad one who killed because of fear and hate. We looked for a new home – and we found *this*.' Her arm swept wide and took in the park and everything beyond it. 'What have you done? What were you thinking, covering the land in a stone that does not breathe, a stone that has no spirit within it? We came here through the Black Wall, and found that everywhere the spirits are dying. And then we found this.'

She pointed towards the haunted house. 'The perfect symbol of your violence. The screams and the pain of a hundred animals dying in fire. Dying because you had put them here for your own *amusement*.'

'Ikari, listen, I accept what you say – but what happened in that fire long ago was an accident.'

'Long ago. Listen, foreigner. That was not long ago. The animals are still screaming – can you not hear them?'

Lechasseur hesitated. Beside him, Mochizuka had started, like a dog hearing a high pitched whistle. It's a trick, he thought. The Kitsune are skilled at mesmerizing human beings . . .

But there was something. A cry, rising and falling, that could almost have been the trumpeting of an elephant. It was followed by the sudden wild, slashing scream of a big cat. The uncanny howling of apes and monkeys. The ugly croaking of carrion birds. Now that he was aware of it, he could not screen it out. It was an invisible menagerie of sounds whirling about him, like scavengers ready for the kill.

The noise, he thought. Mochizuka had said that the screaming of the animals trapped in the fire had been unbearable.

'Look at this,' commanded Ikari. 'The pain is still here. The anger is still here. And now it will stand in judgment upon you. *Hakutaku* is coming.'

There was a sudden jolt to the concrete under their feet, followed by a faint thrumming, as if the ground was a taut string being plucked. The timbers of the haunted house in front of Lechasseur groaned, as they shifted in response to new stresses.

The sounds were increasing, countless animals screeching and chattering, the cacophony of the invisible menagerie surrounding him, growing louder and louder until he had to put his hands over his ears.

'What is it?' Mochizuka cried out, his hands clamped to the sides of his head. 'What kind of animal is that?'

'It's not just one animal,' stated Ikari, disdainfully. 'It's *all the animals.*'

Then, without warning, the haunted house simply blew apart.

Whereas the explosion that had put Lechasseur in a wartime hospital had been quick, this was horrifically slow. The wood of the walls and the roof gave way and sent fragments and jagged splinters spinning across the park, and Lechasseur and Mochizuka threw themselves face down to the ground. A foul wind blew past them, the screams of the frightened, dying beasts carried on the rushing air. The ground shook with the stamping of tremendous feet.

It was Lechasseur's vision. The darkness at the heart of the dead city. It had been here all along.

After the initial explosion, Lechasseur pulled Mochizuka to his feet, and the two men struggled through the unnatural wind to the entrance of the park and under the police tape. Ikari did not attempt to stop or follow them. Lechasseur looked back. All the police officers now had the heads of foxes, eyes glinting in the sunlight, tongues lolling from their grinning jaws as they panted with excitement. Their human hands rested mockingly on their night-sticks and their guns; they didn't need them to look threatening.

Behind them, a dark cloud that had exploded out of the haunted house ballooned straight up into the sky. Looming over the park, it had already begun to assume a shape. A lumpen, rudimentary head. Limbs that were elongating down towards the ground, anchoring the thing to the fabric of the city.

Across the thing's amorphous flank, eyes were opening. Scores of eyes that gazed pitilessly down at the city and its fragile inhabitants.

'*Hakutaku*,' Mochizuka gasped.

10: THE CLOCKS

Lord Nazaeyamon watched Emily's face carefully. Too carefully; she felt like a lab specimen. As he studied her, so she studied him. Marring the perfection of his face was a round depression on the right side of his temple, partially covered over with hair, like the relic of an old wound.

In the chamber's hush, Emily became aware of a sedate, measured ticking all around her, a counterpoint to Mamori's laboured breathing.

The large devices arranged around the sides of the room, she realised, were clocks. They stood on triangular bases of dark, slanted wood. There were tiny sundials of intricate design, half-globe pocket watches, tall, slender candles with regular markings. In one alcove, there was a square, box-like tray holding nothing more than a wooden grill, with sticks of incense arranged above it.

Seeing her glance around, Lord Nazaeyamon smiled. 'This is my collection,' he announced, with relish. 'Usually, before an evil spirit is dispatched back to the hell from which it came, I grant it a last look at my inner sanctum. Because this is the world to come, you see. The sun will shine brightly, and there will be no shadows in which to hide. Do you understand?'

Emily forced herself to look into his eyes and smile. 'What, all because you've learnt how to build a better watch?'

'Yes,' Nazaeyamon replied, gritting his teeth. 'I have these timepieces specially made by watchmakers who are kept confined to a village, east of this compound. Only the Daimyo is allowed to possess a timepiece, and I have sought to make the most of this privilege.'

He smiled. 'I shall divide up the day, like a man divides up an orange into its segments. All the parts will have a name. The common people here change the passage of hours and days with the seasons, as if on a whim; that sort of infantile nonsense will stop. When one of these time-keepers chimes, everyone will think – "Here, now! An hour has gone by." In this way, there shall be a standard time to work, and a standard time to rest, and a precise period in which to do so. Those who do well will be those who understand the new, more accurate methods of the clocks. You see?'

'I think the only thing you'll learn is how fast you're growing old,' Emily said. 'Count time, and see how fast it's slipping away from you.'

'Not as fast as it's slipping away from *you*. No, my dear, once these devices are perfected, there will be new inventions that give us more time. Wheels to transport us, machines to do the work of our arms. And the country's leaders will come to me and say – I *know* that they shall say – "We need something better, Lord Nazaeyamon. Help us."'

'You're not obsessed,' Emily said, disgustedly. 'You're mentally ill. It's you that needs the help.'

At a nod from Nazaeyamon, one of the guards reached forward and grasped Emily's hair. She gasped as her head was yanked backwards.

'This is my gift,' he hissed, pointing to the indentation in the side of his head. 'I barely survived a fall from my father's chariot, when I was a child. The physicians were amazed that someone with such a wound could still function. But I can do more than just function. You see, the mesmerising spells of the Kitsune have no effect on me; this is why I can look on you without a blindfold and retain my senses.' The Daimyo stopped to look at Mamori, to prove his point, before turning back to Emily.

'Now, tell me. I am aware that this wondrous device is a timepiece, and it gives me great joy to add it to my collection.' He held up the wristwatch that had been taken from her. 'But this, I am not sure of. This fetish, this magic square, or whatever it may be.'

He held up the mobile phone and flipped it open, giggling with pleasure at the little tune that sounded. 'Tell me how it works, and I will grant you a death with honour.'

Emily thought hard for a moment. She looked sideways at Mamori, who had her head down, panting silently.

'It is a chronometer and recording device,' she said loudly, 'which is common in the land I come from. I come from your future, my Lord. A land hundreds of years from now.'

Nazaeyamon stared at her with widened eyes. 'What nonsense are you talking, woman?'

'The proof is in the device, my Lord. Do you wish to see how it works? Then press, with your thumb, the button marked "menu" in English. Then click down to number eight, which is marked "data folder". Once you press that, a number of options will be shown. What you are looking for is called "video clip". Or perhaps you would like me to show you?'

Nazaeyamon glared from Emily to the phone, hissing with frustration. 'These markings make no sense to me,' he said, and snapped his fingers at one of the guards. 'Untie her. If she tries anything, kill them both.'

Although the two guards had now drawn their swords and were holding them poised behind her, Emily couldn't resist a little smirk as her bonds were cut. She stood up, rubbing her wrists, trying to conceal the fear and anticipation that were building like a steady drumbeat inside her. Nazaeyamon gingerly handed her the mobile phone, and she took it from him, pressing the controls with a few clicks of her thumb.

The video-clip that she'd recorded back in the twenty-first century flickered into jerky life on the screen.

'I give you the future,' she said, handing it back to the Daimyo, who held it up into the light cast by the candles.

For a long moment, Nazaeyamon stared, his jaw slackening as he tried to take in what he was seeing.

'What? How?'

The Daimyo suddenly gave a high, girlish scream, flinging the mobile phone away from him into the shadows, dropping to his knees and covering his eyes.

'You sorceress, what have you shown me? Is this Hell?'

Emily smoothly reached down, slipped the dagger from the Daimyo's belt and stepped behind him, pressing the weapon against his throat.

'Right,' she yelled. 'Now untie my friend here, or I'll send this clock-watching chump to the Hell he likes to talk about so much. Jump to it!'

'Do as she says!' The Daimyo screamed, a most indecorous tone of fear in his voice.

Crouching down low to get behind the kneeling Nazaeyamon, Emily noticed the two guards exchange glances with each other. Then one of them flicked his eyes to the sliding doors behind them. Oh no, she thought, if they call for reinforcements, we're in even bigger trouble, because they'll be all over us like a bad case of measles. And even if I was prepared to use this oversized toothpick, there's still no way I could get myself, let alone Mamori, out through a whole army.

Before Emily could say another word, the two guards spun round as one, pulling aside the sliding doors with a muffled swish.

The scene beyond the door was a charnel house. The screens were newly painted in bright crimson, several guards lay upon straw matting in the attitudes of sudden and violent demise, and a figure stood above them, his sword glittering cruelly in the dim light, his long hair flowing wildly over his face.

'Judayu,' Emily murmured.

As the two guards moved to protect the Daimyo, Judayu charged forward, the bright steel sweeping forth like an extension of his own hand. One guard went down with an opened chest. The other moved to parry the blow, but a second later, Judayu's sword, moving too fast to see, had skewered his throat.

Gasping and thrashing like a fish, the man collapsed. The metallic stench of blood began to fight with the incense for control of the chamber.

'Lord Nazaeyamon!' Judayu announced. 'My name is Judayu Kokichi, and I apologise for the intrusion. I ask you to die and surrender your head with honour, to pay for the suffering you have caused.'

The only reply was Nazaeyamon's incomprehensible babble of panic, as he broke free from Emily's grasp. He rushed from side to side as Judayu moved forward. Judayu's sword moved like lightning, and then there was a moment's silence as the Daimyo stood there facing the swordsman.

Lord Nazaeyamon's head slowly toppled free from his neck and fell to rest on the floor, eyes staring sightlessly as his beloved clocks continued to mark the passage of time.

'Judayu – ' Emily began.

He held up his hand for silence. 'Hush. I said it was a promise I could not keep. We must go now. There is a trapdoor in the next chamber.'

Emily picked up the mobile phone from where it had been thrown by Lord Nazaeyamon. 'I'm not going without Mamori.'

Judayu moved to the Daimyo's headless body and lifted up the hand to peer at the ornate ring. 'As you must. But we go now, or not at all.'

Mamori looked into Emily's eyes with an unmistakably human expression, as Judayu's sword flashed again.

The wood came away from the gate with a splintering crack.

Judayu stood back to drag the debris away, and before them, the interior of Inari Jinja beckoned. On either side of the blackened shrine, the stone foxes stood guard.

You were brought through the Black Wall in a state of deep hypnosis, Mamori was saying in Emily's head. *The message said to interrogate you, because Ikari had found out you were another time-traveller. Our lair was raided before we had time to communicate. The Black Wall will take us from here to any site of Inari Jinja on the other side that we choose.*

'And you're sure about coming with me?'

The sleek russet head nodded. *I have given my word to help you, as you helped me. You will need navigation through the Wall. And Ikari . . . Time is different on the other side. Ikari has had much time to plan and to act. If what you tell me is true, I must intervene. For the honour of the White Claw Kitsune.*

Emily turned back to Judayu. 'I will be eternally grateful to you.'

'And I to you. The ring that I took from Lord Nazaeyamon, on his severed hand, has been carried to Lord Kaishun. No doubt he and our other neighbours will divide up the estate between them. My fate, and the fate of the village, is uncertain. There will be suffering, that can be assured. But you have shown me . . . ' He paused, looking up at the sun through the trees. 'You have shown me that we cannot hide from change forever. It will come and seek us out.'

'Unless you go and seek it out first.' Emily smiled, and bowed formally to him.

Mamori put her fur-covered hands together and held them in a curious gesture, flexing her fingers once, twice. A dark spot formed in the air. It grew, unfolding itself, layer upon layer opening like an origami flower, the air displacing itself with a *snap, snap, snap*, as the Black Wall took shape.

'Let's go,' said Emily. 'I've got a friend waiting.'

11: THE RABBIT SPEAKS

The *Hakutaku* settled over Sensoji Temple as a boiling cloud of flesh. It swelled upwards, its head becoming more apparent, limbs reaching downwards to the tiny streets and alleyways. Within its dark hide, a thousand appendages flickered into being and then were absorbed back into its growing mass; claws, beaks, wings, feathers, scales and fangs. Scores of eyes burned in its rippling hide.

We've lost, Lechasseur thought, as they ran back to Mochizuka's car. That must be what I saw in the vision, and we couldn't stop it. Everyone's lost.

Around them, pedestrians were stopping in their tracks, motorists were craning their necks out of their cars, people were coming out of the shops to stare.

The panic was slow in starting, but it came. People began to run, the screams building up, towards the river and the subway station.

'What the – who's that?' Lechasseur pushed himself to run faster, as he made out two female figures standing by Mochizuka's car, one of which was waving to them. 'Emily!'

Their embrace was fierce and bittersweet. It was the real Emily, he could tell. He had her smell again; that wonderful, indefinable smell that was truly her.

'I thought I'd lost you,' he grunted.

'Me too.' She lifted up her head, indicating the woman behind her. The stranger seemed oddly familiar. In fact, she looked a lot like Emily

– as if someone had drawn a sketch of Emily, her features, the clothes she wore now, and brought the sketch to life.

'Honoré, she's not human. She's Kitsune.' Seeing his shocked face, she quickly held up her hand for silence. 'Let me tell you where I've been.'

The sky curdled as they exchanged their stories. The creature above them began to spread oily black wings, and lifted its head, outlined in a halo of burning cloud, turning it ponderously to look towards the westerly part of the city.

'So what can we do?' Lechasseur spoke, herding the three of his companions into an alleyway out of the way of the running crowds. Children screamed. Drivers cursed at each other. Several women unfolded parasols and held them over their heads as they hurried along the street. Real funny, Lechasseur thought. That's about as useful as anything I've done.

He turned to Mamori. 'You offered to help, right?'

'That is so.' Her real voice was melodic, and Emily was surprised that it was quite unlike the voice in her head. 'But I am only one. Ikari has all senior brood-members of the clans here.'

'But that thing up there – it was your science that created that.'

'Ikari has had much time to plan. She established her lair here a flight of months ago; she understands this city, she knows how to play with it.'

'What exactly is that thing? What is *Hakutaku*?'

Mamori's face went through a sudden spasm of grimacing, and Lechasseur was reminded how fake her skin really was. 'From what Emily has told me, I believe the seed material that Ikari has put into the clothing enables her to change the shape of the wearer to suit her wishes. Anyone who comes into contact with it, she can control their thoughts, change them into something that human beings will fear, direct them to her purpose.'

She pointed up at the sky. 'The *Hakutaku* is a creation of this land's myth. It is said that it comes from the depths of what you call Hell to this world, in search of villages that have become corrupt. It then destroys those villages and drags the villagers' souls back to Hell with it.'

'Well, that's just swell. So Ikari's used this seed material stuff of yours to create some kind of doomsday machine. And she's using the pain of the animals that died in the fire as fuel for it.'

94

He stared up at the *Hakutaku* in unwilling fascination. It loomed overhead like a mountain, heavy, luxurious tusks gleaming in the sunlight. Ragged tongues from countless mouths licked the wind, and the air was filled with a sound like a titanic beehive.

Possibilities had converged upon this instant; the darkness approaching.

And then, for an absurd moment, something in the creature's fur overhead reminded Lechasseur of the rabbit's foot in his pocket. He looked up again.

If the rabbit could speak, what would it say?

'If I was rabbit,' Mochizuka had said, 'I wouldn't like to eat the grass.' Lechasseur began to feel faint. 'That's it,' he muttered.

'What's it, Honoré?' asked Emily.

'Of course he wouldn't eat grass.' Lechasseur sat down on the pavement, trying to calm the commotion within his skull, 'Because he would still be thinking as a human. If the rabbit could speak, even if it could speak English, we still wouldn't be able to understand it. Because we're not animals. And we have no idea how their minds work. Some people say they don't even have minds.'

He swung round to face them all, scaring them with his sudden, unexpected joy. 'But now we've got Ikari and her Kitsune here. They look like foxes, but they're not foxes. They're not animals, and they're not human. But they've disguised themselves as human. And the point is, they are behaving *just like humans*. Revenge, cruelty, deception; all human traits.'

'Honoré, what are you saying?'

'I'm saying that I'm going to try to stop this. But I'm going to need your help, Mamori. And Mochizuka-san? I have to get something from your car.'

Emily suddenly realised what Lechasseur meant. She clutched at his hand, forcing him to stop.

'No. Honoré. You can't do it. You *can't*.'

'Well, we don't seem to have a lot of choices at the moment, Emily.'

'I won't let you do it.'

And he smiled, that kind, resourceful, determined smile of his, and Emily just wanted to weep.

'I'd like to see you try and stop me.'

Almost complete now, the *Hakutaku* began to flex its limbs experimentally. It had grown ten of them, and it lifted two forelimbs up above the river, as if tasting the air. The city was echoing with the screaming of police and fire engine sirens.

Mochizuka said nothing as he fired up the car engine. Emily watched the reporter from the passenger seat as he navigated a tiny alley that wasn't yet blocked by cars. His jaw was working, but he was sub-vocalising, and she couldn't hear what he was saying. It could have been a prayer to Buddha; it could have been the theme from some TV series running around his head.

He gave the car a final burst of power as they roared through the open gates of the now-deserted Hanayashiki Amusement Park, splitting the police tape asunder, and came to a stop. Ikari and her brood were standing on the wooden bridge, in front of the column of darkness that used to be the ghost house. Ikari was still in human form, and flicked her glossy hair back as she turned to face the new arrivals. The rest of the Kitsune had reverted to their fox-shapes; kimonos in blood-red and black, lips pulled back to show gleaming, curved teeth, furred claws upon the hilts of their ornate swords.

The back door of the car opened and Honoré stepped out.

Ikari watched warily as the tall man strode towards her, his hand held out in a gesture of conciliation.

'Ikari. I am asking you to stop this. I have something to tell you.'

'You have nothing to tell me,' Ikari sneered, raising her arm in a stiff pointing gesture.

Despite herself, Emily gasped as a raging ball of fox-fire struck Honoré's figure and ignited it. He tumbled backwards, limned in flames and smoke.

So quick, Emily thought. She didn't even hesitate. Ikari and her brood were smiling as they approached Honoré's smoking, prone body.

They stopped as the body got slowly to its feet and faced Ikari once more.

The woman's smile disappeared as Honoré's face and body fragmented, the image splitting and sliding away to reveal what lay beneath.

Mamori. In her true form. She crouched down to balance on her wooden sandals, her kimono a swirl of willow and lotus-flowers. She was panting with excitement and pain, her glistening eyes a direct challenge to Ikari. The White Claw Kitsune turned to their leader in confusion.

There was a steady susurration in Emily's skull, which meant that the Kitsune were talking to each other. She could not separate the words, but there was shock there, shock and a growing sense of disappointment. Some kind of challenge had been issued.

And then something black and sleek hit Ikari from behind.

'Oh Honoré,' Emily muttered, her knuckles pressed against her mouth. 'What are you doing?'

The thing that had knocked Ikari down and pinned her to the ground now reared its head.

Its head was covered in sleek, dark fur, light glittering from its whiskers and moist nose. Its pointed white teeth were bared as a threat, dangerously close to Ikari's throat. Its furred, heavy tail pounded the Hanayashiki pavement, warning off the other Kitsune who stood, dazed, nearby.

The creature looked like an otter in the shape of a man. The shape of Honoré Lechasseur, in fact, wearing a Hide and Chic jacket, which Mamori had 'reprogrammed', as she had described the process.

'A question,' the Honoré-thing asked. 'A race that kills indiscriminately. A race that, in its arrogance, thinks it is the dominant life form. A race that kills other species not for necessity, out of hunger, but for sport. Is it your opinion that such a race has any right to exist?'

Never, snarled the voice in Emily's skull, breaking through the background noise. *Such a race is worthless. Beyond any hope of redemption.*

'Do you swear it in front of your brood?' interjected Mamori.

'I so swear.' Ikari looked at the female Kitsune. 'So why are you helping such a race? You have seen what the humans have done to our world.'

'I am not talking of the humans.' Honoré stood upon his back legs, raising himself up to his full height and bringing Ikari up with him, one furred arm held firmly around her neck. 'I am talking of *you*!'

The Kitsune-warriors drew closer, but they were not attacking; they were listening.

'You have been here too long, Ikari,' Honoré continued. 'You have spent your time here planning revenge, and toying with other life-forms for your own pleasure. That is the human way of doing things. You have betrayed your own kind.'

'You have broken the laws of your own brood, Ikari,' Mamori said. 'Have you forgotten what we said as we planned together in the woods?'

'This is justice, Mamori!'

'Really?' snarled the man-animal, not relaxing its grip on Ikari for a second. 'Then why the endless charade? Why the endless shifting of identities? Why are you wearing your woman-shell *even now*, Ikari?'

'You have lost yourselves,' added Mamori. 'You have forgotten what it is to be Kitsune, and adopted the worst of what it is to be human.'

'The great spirit's jaws!' cried Ikari. 'We are not human! We are *more* than human!'

'Perhaps. But *you* are less than Kitsune.' Honoré suddenly released Ikari, spinning her round to face him. Displaying his brutal claws in front of her face, he slowly sheathed them.

'Recall the *Hakutaku*, and all of your senseless traps. Leave here. This is not your home. You would have to exterminate every single human on this planet, because if you did not, they would exterminate *you* like the vermin you have behaved as. You think you have seen human cruelty? You have seen nothing.'

'Accept the truth,' Mamori pleaded. 'We cannot live in the same space.'

'Use your science to find a new home,' Lechasseur finished. 'And then find *yourself*.'

Ikari looked up at them both. The change began slowly. Her smooth, faultless face suddenly split into dozens of lines, a cobweb of cracks following her cheeks and the bones underneath, as her human face melted away to reveal the glory of her true Kitsune face.

'I so swear,' she declared.

In front of the Hanayashiki Amusement Park, Honoré Lechasseur and Emily Blandish sat on the pavement and watched the sky. The Hide and Chic jacket lay discarded in a nearby rubbish bin.

The transformation had been slow at first. The *Hakutaku* had continued to hover over Askausa, staring accusingly at all below. But it had lost its animating intelligence. Now it just drifted, as gently as a cloud, and gradually, rips and rents appeared in its hide, to let the sun shine through. The *Hakutaku* was dissolving back into the formless chaos from which it had been conjured.

Mamori had left fifteen minutes earlier, with the silent Ikari and her brood, again wearing their human faces and melting into the confused crowd of Japanese onlookers.

Mochizuka was already jabbering on his mobile phone to his editor.

'So this guy Judayu kills the Daimyo and cuts off his head,' Honoré was summarising. 'So at least that takes the pressure off the Kitsune.'

'Yes, but Mamori's seen the future. She knows that the humans will tip the balance in their favour.'

Lechasseur sighed. Emily peered closely at his face. No sign of fur or whiskers; and his hands were back to their normal, reassuring shape.

'So what was it like?'

'What was what like?'

'Being an animal.'

Lechasseur shrugged. 'Just as confusing as being a human, I'd say.'

The mini-mall that had been the flagship of Hide and Chic stood before them. The gleaming edifice of steel, glass and chrome was totally gone. In its place was a drab, ageing building with cracked, white-plaster walls, ugly air-conditioning units and electrical cables crusting its exterior, a rash of overgrown ivy covering one entire wall.

The nearby shrine to Inari-sama, however, remained unchanged.

'*Kore wa abura-age desu,*' Mochizuka said. He held out three paper-wrapped bundles in his hands. 'Vinegar rice, with soy-sauce and sugar flavour, wrapped in tofu shell.'

He, Emily and Lechasseur each took a bundle, bowed low, and placed it in front of the collection box. The stone foxes watched them impassively from either side. Mochizuka clapped his hands twice. '*Yoroshiku onegai shimasu.*'

Emily raised a hand experimentally. It's gone, she thought. The Black Walls have closed.

They turned to leave. Outside, the noise of the traffic was unceasing; people walked by on the pavement, ignoring everything as usual.

'So what are you planning to do now, Mochizuka-san?' asked Emily.

'My editor and I have plan,' the journalist began to explain. 'We have been consultation with police and national government, and we will publish an interesting story.' Mochizuka cleared his throat.

'Tokyo is suffered attack from religious cult. Cult set up false company, known as Hide and Chic. That same cult released drug around Tokyo, to give hallucination and to make scared people to become to want to join their cult. Last hallucination was massive animal in sky above

Asakusa. Massive animal was cloud of dangerous nerve agent which had explosion.' Mochizuka beamed.

'How do you think?'

'A religious cult scaring people into joining them by giving them drugs, and then planning a terrorist attack on their own country?' Lechasseur shook his head in resignation. 'I'm sorry, that's just too whacked out, nobody's going to believe that.'

Mochizuka grinned shyly. 'We are national magazine. We say, people believe.'

Emily returned his grin. 'Well, I'm sure it will be okay.' She reached up and kissed him on the cheek. They all bowed to each other, and then, laughing, shook hands.

'You want ride to airport?'

'No thanks, you've been too kind. I'm sure we'll manage somehow – won't we, Honoré?'

The sun continues to shine and the cicadas fill the air with their never-ending hum. Akihira Noguchi stands in the shadow of the wisteria tree, the rake in his hand.

The rake moves and the gravel moves with it. The tiny grains of stone, as fine as sand, are swept into new patterns, their old patterns destroyed.

The two foreigners have just left again, after stopping by to say farewell. They thanked him profusely for his help, but they really needn't have. He knows that they have something to do with the bizarre news stories coming out of Tokyo; revelations and accusations concerning Aoyama and Asakusa. Stories that verge on the incredible; but then, Tokyo never was a place that a person should take too seriously.

Noguchi leans on his rake, looking at his garden of waves and shadows. The stones, he knows, will one day be worn down to gravel; and the patterns that he makes today with the rake will be swept away by the rain and the wind. But for a time, the patterns remain, and with care and attention, they can be moved and shaped into forms that are pleasing and good.

ABOUT THE AUTHOR

John Paul Catton lives and works in Tokyo, where he teaches English language and literature. He has worked freelance for various magazines in Japan, the UK and the USA, including *Metropolis*, *Tokyo Eye Ai* and *The London Time Out Guide to Tokyo*. His short fiction and comic strips have appeared in *Roadworks*, *Terror Tales*, *Xenos* among others, and he has a regular column appear in the magazine *The 3rd Alternative*.

ACKNOWLEDGEMENTS

Thank you to the *Time Out*, *Optia* and *East West* crews for all the advice and beer, thank you to my wife Minako and her family for showing me the Tokyo that hides behind the bright lights, and a great big thank you to my long-suffering family in the UK.

TIME HUNTER

A range of high-quality, original paperback novellas featuring the adventures in time of Honoré Lechasseur. Part mystery, part detective story, part dark fantasy, part science fiction . . . these books are guaranteed to enthral fans of good fiction everywhere, and are in the spirit of our acclaimed range of *Doctor Who* Novellas.

ALREADY AVAILABLE:

THE WINNING SIDE by LANCE PARKIN
Emily is dead! Killed by an unknown assailant. Honoré and Emily find themselves caught up in a plot reaching from the future to their past, and with their very existence, not to mention the future of the entire world, at stake, can they unravel the mystery before it is too late?
An adventure in time and space.
£7.99 (+ £1.50 UK p&p) Standard p/b ISBN 1-903889-35-9 (pb)
£25.00 (+ £1.50 UK p&p) Deluxe h/b ISBN 1-903889-36-7 (hb)

THE TUNNEL AT THE END OF THE LIGHT by STEFAN PETRUCHA
In the heart of post-war London, a bomb is discovered lodged at a disused station between Green Park and Hyde Park Corner. The bomb detonates, and as the dust clears, it becomes apparent that *something* has been awakened. Strange half-human creatures attack the workers at the site, hungrily searching for anything containing sugar . . .

Meanwhile, Honoré and Emily are contacted by eccentric poet Randolph Crest, who believes himself to be the target of these subterranean creatures. The ensuing investigation brings Honoré and Emily up against a terrifying force from deep beneath the earth, and one which even with their combined powers, they may have trouble stopping.
An adventure in time and space.
£7.99 (+ £1.50 UK p&p) Standard p/b ISBN 1-903889-37-5 (pb)
£25.00 (+ £1.50 UK p&p) Deluxe h/b ISBN 1-903889-38-3 (hb)

THE CLOCKWORK WOMAN by CLAIRE BOTT
Honoré and Emily find themselves imprisoned in the 19th Century by

a celebrated inventor . . . but help comes from an unexpected source – a humanoid automaton created by and to give pleasure to its owner. As the trio escape to London, they are unprepared for what awaits them, and at every turn it seems impossible to avert what fate may have in store for the Clockwork Woman.

An adventure in time and space.

£7.99 (+ £1.50 UK p&p) Standard p/b ISBN 1-903889-39-1 (pb)
£25.00 (+ £1.50 UK p&p) Deluxe h/b ISBN 1-903889-40-5 (hb)

COMING SOON

THE SEVERED MAN by GEORGE MANN

An adventure in time and space.

£7.99 (+ £1.50 UK p&p) Standard p/b ISBN 1-903889-43-X (pb)
£25.00 (+ £1.50 UK p&p) Deluxe h/b ISBN 1-903889-44-8 (hb)

PUB: DECEMBER 2004 (UK)

TIME HUNTER FILM:

DAEMOS RISING by DAVID J HOWE
directed by KEITH BARNFATHER

Daemos Rising is a sequel to both the *Doctor Who* adventure *The Daemons* and to *Downtime*, an earlier drama featuring the Yeti. It is also a prequel of sorts to Telos Publishing's *Time Hunter* series. It stars Miles Richardson as ex-UNIT operative Douglas Cavendish, and Beverley Cressman as Brigadier Lethbridge-Stewart's daughter Kate. Trapped in an isolated cottage, Cavendish thinks he is seeing ghosts. The only person who might understand and help is Kate Lethbridge-Stewart . . . but when she arrives, she realises that Cavendish is key in a plot to summon the Daemons back to the Earth. With time running out, Kate discovers that sometimes even the familiar can turn out to be your worst nightmare. Also starring Andrew Wisher, and featuring Ian Richardson as the Narrator.

An adventure in time and space.

£12.00 (+ £2.50 UK p&p) VHS; £14.00 (+ £2.50 UK p&p) DVD
Order direct from Reeltime Pictures, PO Box 23435, London SE26 5WU

HORROR/FANTASY

CAPE WRATH by PAUL FINCH
Death and horror on a deserted Scottish island as an ancient Viking warrior chief returns to life.
£8.00 (+ £1.50 UK p&p) Standard p/b ISBN: 1-903889-60-X

KING OF ALL THE DEAD by STEVE LOCKLEY & PAUL LEWIS
The king of all the dead will have what is his.
£8.00 (+ £1.50 UK p&p) Standard p/b ISBN: 1-903889-61-8

GUARDIAN ANGEL by STEPHANIE BEDWELL-GRIME
Devilish fun as Guardian Angel Porsche Winter loses a soul to the devil . . .
£9.99 (+ £2.50 UK p&p) Standard p/b ISBN: 1-903889-62-6

ASPECTS OF A PSYCHOPATH by ALISTAIR LANGSTON
Goes deeper than ever before into the twisted psyche of a serial killer. Horrific, graphic and gripping, this book is not for the squeamish.
£8.00 (+ £1.50 UK p&p) Standard p/b ISBN: 1-903889-63-4

SPECTRE by STEPHEN LAWS
The inseparable Byker Chapter: six boys, one girl, growing up together in the back streets of Newcastle. Now memories are all that Richard Eden has left, and one treasured photograph. But suddenly, inexplicably, the images of his companions start to fade, and as they vanish, so his friends are found dead and mutilated. Something is stalking the Chapter, picking them off one by one, something connected with their past, and with the girl they used to know.
£9.99 (+ £2.50 UK p&p) Standard p/b ISBN: 1-903889-72-3
£30.00 (+ £2.50 UK p&p) Deluxe h/b ISBN: 1-903889-73-1

THE HUMAN ABSTRACT by GEORGE MANN
A future tale of private detectives, AIs, Nanobots, love and death.
£7.99 (+ £1.50 UK p&p) Standard p/b ISBN: 1-903889-65-0

BREATHE by CHRISTOPHER FOWLER
The Office meets *Night of the Living Dead*.

£7.99 (+ £1.50 UK p&p) Standard p/b ISBN: 1-903889-67-7
£25.00 (+ £1.50 UK p&p) Deluxe h/b ISBN: 1-903889-68-5

HOUDINI'S LAST ILLUSION by STEVE SAVILE
Can the master illusionist Harry Houdini outwit the dead shades of his past?
£7.99 (+ £1.50 UK p&p) Standard p/b ISBN: 1-903889-66-9

ALICE'S JOURNEY BEYOND THE MOON by RJ CARTER
A sequel to the classic Lewis Carroll tales.
£6.99 (+ £1.50 UK p&p) Standard p/b ISBN: 1-903889-76-6
£30.00 (+ £1.50 UK p&p) Deluxe h/b ISBN: 1-903889-77-4

TV/FILM GUIDES

A DAY IN THE LIFE: THE UNOFFICIAL AND UNAUTHORISED GUIDE TO 24 by KEITH TOPPING
Complete episode guide to the first season of the popular TV show.
£9.99 (+ £2.50 p&p) Standard p/b ISBN: 1-903889-53-7

THE TELEVISION COMPANION: THE UNOFFICIAL AND UN-AUTHORISED GUIDE TO DOCTOR WHO by DAVID J HOWE & STEPHEN JAMES WALKER
Complete episode guide to the popular TV show.
£14.99 (+ £4.75 UK p&p) Standard p/b ISBN: 1-903889-51-0

LIBERATION: THE UNOFFICIAL AND UNAUTHORISED GUIDE TO BLAKE'S 7 by ALAN STEVENS & FIONA MOORE
Complete episode guide to the popular TV show.
Featuring a foreword by David Maloney
£9.99 (+ £2.50 UK p&p) Standard p/b ISBN: 1-903889-54-5

HOWE'S TRANSCENDENTAL TOYBOX: SECOND EDITION by DAVID J HOWE & ARNOLD T BLUMBERG
Complete guide to *Doctor Who* Merchandise.
£25.00 (+ £4.75 UK p&p) Standard p/b ISBN: 1-903889-56-1

HOWE'S TRANSCENDENTAL TOYBOX: 2003 EDITION by DAVID J HOWE & ARNOLD T BLUMBERG

Complete guide to *Doctor Who* Merchandise released in 2003.
£7.99 (+ £1.50 UK p&p) Standard p/b ISBN: 1-903889-57-X

A VAULT OF HORROR by KEITH TOPPING

A Guide to 80 Classic (and not so classic) British Horror Films.
£12.99 (+ £4.75 UK p&p) Standard p/b ISBN: 1-903889-58-8

HANK JANSON

Classic pulp crime thrillers from the 1940s and 1950s.

TORMENT by HANK JANSON

£9.99 (+ £1.50 UK p&p) Standard p/b ISBN: 1-903889-80-4

WOMEN HATE TILL DEATH by HANK JANSON

£9.99 (+ £1.50 UK p&p) Standard p/b ISBN: 1-903889-81-2

SOME LOOK BETTER DEAD by HANK JANSON

£9.99 (+ £1.50 UK p&p) Standard p/b ISBN: 1-903889-82-0

SKIRTS BRING ME SORROW by HANK JANSON

£9.99 (+ £1.50 UK p&p) Standard p/b ISBN: 1-903889-83-9

WHEN DAMES GET TOUGH by HANK JANSON

£9.99 (+ £1.50 UK p&p) Standard p/b ISBN: 1-903889-85-5

ACCUSED by HANK JANSON

£9.99 (+ £1.50 UK p&p) Standard p/b ISBN: 1-903889-86-3

THE TRIALS OF HANK JANSON by STEVE HOLLAND

£12.99 (+ £2.50 UK p&p) Standard p/b ISBN: 1-903889-84-7

Ordering details overleaf

The prices shown are correct at time of going to press. However, the publishers reserve the right to increase prices from those previously advertised without prior notice.

TELOS PUBLISHING
c/o Beech House, Chapel Lane, Moulton, Cheshire, CW9 8PQ, England
Email: orders@telos.co.uk • Web: www.telos.co.uk

To order copies of any Telos books, please visit our website where there are full details of all titles and facilities for worldwide credit card online ordering, or send a cheque or postal order (UK only) for the appropriate amount (including postage and packing), together with details of the book(s) you require, plus your name and address to the above address. Overseas readers please send two international reply coupons for details of prices and postage rates.